MW00915826

Brothers in Blue: Max

Brothers in Blue
Book 1

Jeanne St. James

Editor: Molly Daniels
Cover Artist: EmCat Designs

www.jeannestjames.com

Sign up for my newsletter for insider information, author news, and new releases:
www.jeannestjames.com/newslettersignup

Keep an eye on her website at http://www.jeannestjames.com/or sign up for her newsletter to learn about her upcoming releases: http://www.jeannestjames.com/newslettersignup

Author Links: Instagram * Facebook * Goodreads Author Page * Newsletter * Jeanne's Review & Book Crew * BookBub * TikTok * YouTube

Dedication

To my own personal man in uniform,
thank you for being the calm to my storm.

Chapter One

For forty-five minutes the little red rental sat in the parking lot. Amanda Barber remained frozen in the driver's seat. She stared through the windshield at the brick building in front of her. The car's engine was off, the keys still hanging in the ignition. It wouldn't take much for her to reach out, turn them, and go back the way she had come.

She read the sign on the building one more time as if reading it would put off the inevitable. Howell's Adult Day Care.

It was getting dark; she couldn't sit there anymore. She had promised her stepmother's attorney that she would stick around for a couple weeks. Just a couple of weeks. Fourteen days. Half a month.

She had to stop being a wimp.

Okay, no more hesitation. She grabbed the keys and tossed them into her purse. She had to get this over with. She left the car and went into the building before she could change her mind.

As the door closed behind her with a *click* that sounded deafening to her own ears, Amanda glanced around. A few older people sat knitting, reading, and talking in small groups. A television droned in the background. A very elderly gentleman sat in a wheelchair in front of a large picture window, his head bobbing as he dozed off.

A woman, just a few years older than her, looked up and spotted Amanda. A frown creasing her forehead, the woman straightened from helping the young man who was sitting at a card table. Amanda wasn't quite sure what the young man needed help doing. It looked as though he'd been drawing. The woman leaned over and said something in his ear before approaching Amanda.

"Can I help you?"

"I guess so."

A puzzled look crossed the woman's face when Amanda didn't continue.

The woman prodded, "Do you need information? Or a tour of our facility?"

"No."

The woman squinted in confusion and tilted her head with an unspoken question. As she opened her mouth, Amanda interrupted her. "I'm here for Gregory Barber."

She must have said it loud enough, as the young man at the table lifted his head from his project and turned toward them. He laughed loudly and brushed away the hair that fell into his eyes with the back of his bent wrist.

An O formed on the woman's lips. "You must be Amanda."

Amanda frowned. Of course the woman knew who she was. She bet all of Manning Grove had been waiting for her to show up.

"Yes, I'm here to pick up Greg."

Amanda bit her lip as the young man rose from the table with a crooked smile. Next thing she knew, he was running toward her, his arms flailing in the air. Amanda automatically stepped back. She really wanted to turn and run, but the young man's arms wrapped around her, squeezing her until she couldn't breathe.

The woman grabbed his arms, trying to peel him off. "Greg! Greg! Let her go."

Greg rocked Amanda back and forth, pressing his head into her chest, squeezing her even tighter. She groaned in pain.

"Greg!"

"Donna, is this 'Manda? Is this 'Manda?" His booming voice vibrated against her chest.

"Greg, you're going to squeeze her to death."

Greg reluctantly let her go and stepped back, the crooked smile on his face even larger. A bit of spit sprayed out of his mouth as he yelled, "My sister 'Manda!"

"Yes, Greg, your sister is here to pick you up." Donna turned to Amanda. "As you can guess by now, I'm Donna. I manage this facility." Concern crossed her face. "You look pale. Do you want to sit down?"

Amanda shook her head. "No." She took a deep breath, rubbing her ribs, checking for damage. She pulled down her skirt and adjusted the sweater that was askew under her jacket. "No, I'm okay."

"Are you taking Greg back to his mother's house?"

"Yes."

"Have you ever dealt with a special needs person before?"

Amanda looked at Greg, who stared back at her with the biggest grin on his face. "No." Greg couldn't stand still; he was fidgeting about and mumbling to himself.

Donna frowned. "Oh boy."

Amanda didn't want to hear that. *Oh boy.* What did that mean? She knew that she would be in over her head. But *"Oh boy?"*

Shit.

"Uh, is he ready to go?"

Donna looked at Greg. "Yes. He's very excited to meet his sister, as you can see." She returned her attention to Amanda and lifted her eyebrows. "This is for the first time, right?"

Amanda nodded. She didn't know whether to be ashamed or afraid. Shame was quickly clouding her feeling of fear. She had no doubt that Donna knew the answer to that question before she had even asked it. Amanda was sure that the whole town knew the truth.

Double shit.

Donna grabbed her arm, pity in her eyes. "Look. I'll give you my card. If you have any problems or questions, call me. Greg's a good kid; he's easy to work with, easy to please."

Amanda looked at the person in question. He was no kid. Her half-brother was twenty-two years old. Twenty-two.

Old enough to drink, vote, join the Army.

An adult who only acted like a child.

"Thanks. I might take you up on that offer."

Donna smiled for the first time. "I'm sure you will. Here is a brochure on my facility and my card. Greg comes here three days a week. A bus will pick him up before eight a.m. on Mondays, Wednesday, and Fridays, except for holidays. A bus will drop him off after six p.m."

Amanda's head was spinning. "Okay."

"Greg, are you ready to go now?"

"Yep. Yep. Yep. I'm ready to go." Greg hopped on one foot, then the other, in his excitement. "We's going now!" He ran up to Amanda again and held out his twisted hand.

Amanda reached out and grabbed it. His huge grin was irresistible. She gave him a weak smile back. "Ready, Bud?"

"Who's Bud?"

Amanda looked at her brother. He might be only a half-brother, but he was still blood. He was family. Amanda relaxed her stiff muscles a bit and gave his hand a squeeze. "You are, Bud. You are going to be my new best bud."

"Oh! Oh! Donna, I'm Bud! I'm a Bud!" Greg started to pull her toward the door.

"Oh wait, Ms. Barber!" Amanda's head turned toward Donna as she was being tugged out through the entranceway. "Don't forget Chaos."

"What?" She grabbed the doorjamb to keep Greg from dragging her out the door and bouncing her over the pavement in his enthusiasm.

"Chaos," she repeated as if that clarified everything.

Donna went to the back door and held it open. A black-and-white border collie bounded through the door and circled them, barking, just as out of control as Greg.

Chaos.

How appropriate.

———

Keys jingled and hinges squeaked as Amanda opened the front door of her new home.

New temporary home, she reminded herself.

Due to the long flight followed by the boring, long drive to this *in-the-middle-of-nowhere* town, she was exhausted. She needed to get a good night's sleep so she could think clearly in the morning.

She glanced at her watch. Seven.

Neither Greg nor she had had dinner yet, and here she was, thinking about going to bed. Like an old maid. In Miami the nightlife hadn't even begun yet.

Chaos brushed past her. The dog probably needed to be fed too.

"Greg, do you know how to feed Chaos?"

When there was no answer, Amanda turned to look at him. He was still standing near the car. He had been suspiciously calm and quiet as they drove into the neighborhood and up to the house. The excited "boy" was gone.

"Greg?"

"Is Mama in there?"

Even in the dark and him being so far away from her, the sadness and confusion was clearly recognizable on his face. But his question made the hairs on the back of her neck rise.

"No, Greg, your mama is gone. Come on. I need to make you some dinner."

"Mama makes good food."

Amanda sighed. She didn't want to deal with this. He wasn't her responsibility. She had never even met her brother before today. She knew he existed, but they'd lived in different worlds. Her world had never included her father, her stepmother, or her half-brother. Amanda's mother, Anne, had made sure of that.

"Hey, Bud, I might not be the best cook. In fact, I'm probably one of the worst. But I can sure make a bowl of soup and a mean grilled cheese sandwich."

His new nickname seemed to perk him up a bit. He reluctantly followed behind her into the house.

Amanda ran her hand along the wall, since the house was pitch-dark, looking for a light switch. Her fingers located one, and she flipped the lights on. The house was cute. And small. Everything seemed to have a place, and it was really neat. And despite the fact that her stepmother Dolores had died over a week ago, the house seemed relatively clean.

The living room to her right was comfortable looking with a big, soft couch and a few beautifully carved, old, but heavy wood tables. Antiques, probably. Most of the decorations on the wall were framed photos. She would look closer at them later. After she got some sleep.

One thing Amanda quickly noticed was that there was nothing delicate. No pottery or glass or even small knickknacks. Amanda could imagine why when she heard a crash. She rushed back toward the rear of the house.

The large kitchen was modern with all updated stainless steel appliances and gorgeous granite countertops. A copper pot rack hung over an island, which surrounded by dark wooden stools.

And in the center of that beautiful kitchen was Greg with a sheepish look on his face. "Sorry."

He had dropped Chaos's metal bowl, but the dog didn't care. As fast as he could eat, the dog vacuumed up every last kibble wherever they had rolled.

"It's okay, Bud. Now let's find something for you to eat."

After a few minutes of searching cabinets, she put together a quick dinner for Greg, and as he ate, she explored the house some more. Even though the house was small, like she first thought, it was comfy. It was a two story with three bedrooms and two bathrooms.

The kitchen had to be one of the biggest rooms in the house. The backyard was long and narrow, adequately fenced for the dog. The part Amanda loved the most was the sunroom that appeared to have been recently added to the deck in the back.

Amanda returned to the kitchen to check on Greg. Maybe she shouldn't have left him for so long. Or at least should have given him a napkin. As she helped him wipe the tomato soup off his clothes, she quizzed him, trying to find out what he could do and not do.

Around ten p.m., after Greg watched, according to him, one of his "favorite" programs, she went up with him to his room.

"I see you're a NASCAR fan, Greg."

"Love NASCAR. Love racing! I'm gonna be a race car driver."

"Let me guess. Tony Stewart is your favorite driver."

Greg squealed excitedly. "How'd you know?"

Amanda looked around the bedroom, which was full of the number fourteen posters, model cars, and memorabilia. She pulled down the Stewart bedspread. *Hmm, how did she know?*

"Can you take it from here? Can you get ready for bed?"

"Yep."

"Okay, night, Greg."

"'Manda?"

"Yes?"

"Can I get a hug?"

"You bet, Bud." His hug wasn't so bone crushing this time. "Night, Buddy. I'll see you in the morning."

"Night, 'Manda."

Amanda headed back downstairs. She went directly to the white envelope that the lawyer had given her, where she had left it on the kitchen counter earlier. She grabbed it and went into the sunroom. She sank with a tired groan into the plush love seat and ripped it open. Chaos ran in and jumped up, curling next to her. Amanda smoothed a hand down his silky back.

She unfolded the letter and began to read.

Dear Amanda,

I know we never met, and I regret that. Nothing can change that now. First thing I want you to know is that your father loved you, no matter what you thought. He made a good life for us, and for that I'm grateful. I loved him very much.

I know that this must be a big shock for you, meeting your brother for the first time. Gregory is a good boy. I hope you'll see that for yourself.

It's been tough for Greg after your father died from that heart attack two years ago. Not to mention me. I know it's going to be even tougher for Greg after I go. Greg has no idea that I was diagnosed with breast cancer. I don't think he'd understand it anyway.

If you're reading this, then Greg has lost both of his parents. I hope you find it in your heart to help him and love him. I know he's only your half-brother, but he's still your brother. You're all he has.

Please look deep within yourself to open your heart to him. It's not an easy job. Gregory can take care of himself somewhat, but he needs a lot of guidance. I was trying to get him to be more independent, but he will never be able to live on his own. He really needs you. I don't want him to end up in a home, alone.

The house is yours now, along with a trust that your father and I had set up in which you will receive monthly income to help take care of Gregory. It should be enough that if you stay in Manning Grove, you should be able to not work and be there for Greg when he needs you. If you take him back to Miami (I hope you won't), it probably won't last long at all.

This is a great town and the people are friendly and they know Gregory. I know this might not convince you, but I don't think Gregory would be happy in a big city.

I'm babbling now...

Amanda read through a "grocery list" of what tasks Greg could do on his own and what he needed help with. She crushed the letter in her hand and threw it across the room. It bounced off a lamp and landed in the middle of the floor.

Chaos leaped off the chair and retrieved the "ball" before ceremoniously dropping it back in her lap. She glared at him and the crumpled, damp letter, trying not to scream. Struggling not to cry.

She didn't want to do this. She couldn't do this. This woman had no right to ask her. She never asked for a brother. Never cared that she was an only child. Her mother had spoiled her. Not because she loved Amanda, but because she wanted to control her and, when necessary, keep Amanda out of her hair.

Chaos nudged her hand, waiting for her to throw the "ball" again.

Staring at the black-and-white dog, she realized that she was expected to be responsible. *Her*—Amanda Barber! She who had never even owned a pet. Not even a hamster. Now she was actually responsible for another human being. It was too much.

She'd let Greg down.

Her head dropped into her hands, and she lost it. Sobs racked her body until her stomach ached, her nose was stuffy and swollen, and her eyes puffy. She sniffled loudly. Chaos sat at her feet, ears perked, and tilted his head up at her with a silent inquiry.

She was scared.

And alone.

Not even her mother could—or would—help.

The thought strengthened her. She didn't need her mother. Her mother was angry with her. She had said that Amanda would never be able to do it. That she was incapable.

Amanda would show her. She would be better than her mother. Greg was her blood. Her family. She would be caring, warm, and loving.

At least she could try.

Chaos, tired of waiting, jumped back up beside her. Amanda's hand stroked his head. She was determined to prove her mother wrong.

Chapter Two

THE EXCITED BARKING of a dog awakened Amanda. Her back was stiff as she slowly and painfully unfolded herself from the love seat. She didn't remember falling asleep in the chair late last night. Her clothes were disheveled and wrinkled, her shoes gone.

Through the sunroom's expanse of windows, Amanda saw why. Chaos was busy tossing one in the air and catching it. The other was already half-buried in a hole in the middle of the yard.

Fuck! They had cost her three hundred dollars. Almost a week's worth of tips from bartending.

The screech of chair legs against linoleum caught her attention, and she decided to ignore the dog. For now. She was sure Chaos would give her shoes a proper burial later. She hurried into the kitchen to see her new responsibility sitting at the table.

Greg's hair was standing up on one side of his head, and he was decked out in a SpongeBob SquarePants T-shirt and a pair of white cotton briefs. And that was all.

He looked up at Amanda as she stepped into the room. He gave her a wide grin, a piece of cereal stuck to the corner of his mouth.

"I made my own breakfast, 'Manda!"

Amanda groaned. "I see."

What she saw was a box of Honey O's spilled all over the table and an overflowing cereal bowl. Luckily the quart of milk was still upright, but white drops dotted the floor and table. And Greg himself. The worst part was that he was using an enormous serving spoon to eat from.

With every scoop into the overloaded bowl, the combination of milk and cereal sloshed over the side.

She quickly searched for the utensil drawer. As soon as she found them, she handed her brother a normal-sized spoon. "Here, use this, Bud."

Greg eyed the normal spoon and shook his head. "No. I like this one." He attempted to shove the oversize spoon into his mouth and milk dripped down his chin. She hastily grabbed a napkin to wipe his face.

A nurse and a maid...that's what she'd become. A nursemaid.

But this morning, the anger just wouldn't come. She couldn't help but reach out and attempt to smooth down his unruly hair.

"What's Chaos doin'?"

"He found some new toys. You stay here and finish your breakfast. I'm going to wander around the house a little bit. Okay?"

Greg couldn't care less. He was engrossed with the puzzles on the back of the cereal box.

Amanda wanted to see the house again in the light of day. She went up to stake out the master bedroom and made use of the single bathroom upstairs. Then she wandered back down through the main floor and passed Greg, who was having a deep conversation with himself—while still eating—on her way out to the garage.

She flipped on the light. In the single-car garage sat an older Buick. She pressed the garage door opener to get a better view.

Once the sunshine flooded in, she walked around the cramped garage, inspecting the car. It was gray. Four door. The perfect car for a grandparent.

Boring.

Just like living in this town was going to be.

When she rounded the back of the car, she stopped in horror. The license plate read GREGSMOM. She groaned. She absolutely refused to drive around town with that plate.

She looked up as Greg stepped into the garage. Still in his underwear and milk-stained tee.

"We goin' for a ride?" His hands twisted in ways that she never could have imagined possible, and his arms jerked with excitement.

"Not like that you're not." She lifted a brow toward his attire and didn't know if he'd understand or not.

But he did. His smile got even bigger as he bounced on his toes. "Oh...oh...oh! I'm gonna go dress!" He stomped up the two steps into the house, and Amanda could hear a squeal of delight as well as what sounded like a herd of elephants pounding up to the second floor.

Now she just needed to clean herself up. She closed the garage door. She would take the rental. The rental car company wasn't coming until four o'clock to pick it up anyway.

As she had done the previous day when she met with her stepmother's lawyer, Amanda had parked the little red coupe in the public lot in town. She and Greg had spent a couple of hours walking, checking out the various mom-and-pop stores along Main Street. Since it was a Saturday, it seemed busier than what she imagined it would be. Every store they went into, someone would yell out a greeting to Greg and he would yell back, more often than not, directly in Amanda's ear.

Amanda was amazed at Greg's skill of knowing everyone by name, since she was terrible at it. It was quite a gift for him, especially considering this morning he couldn't even remember to put on a pair of pants. Everyone seemed to know him in town and treated him kindly.

After buying him a cone of mint chocolate chip ice cream and a large mocha latte for herself from the Coffee and Cream shop on the corner, they wandered back through the square and into the dollar store. There, she bought an armful of new chew toys for Chaos. Greg had a ball picking them out for his dog and kept repeating, "Everything's just one dollar!" Finally, Amanda had to drag him out of there before her head exploded. Even the caffeine-laden latte couldn't get rid of the full-blown headache she had.

As they left the dollar store, Greg suddenly grabbed her hand, almost knocking out the shopping bag. He started pulling her down the sidewalk: a boy on a mission.

Today she had on her one-hundred-and-fifty-dollar pair of boots, the ones with a slight heel that went perfect with the pair of skinny jeans and dark purple leather jacket she was wearing. But even in low heels, he was dragging her way too fast.

"Hold up, Greg! I can't walk that fast."

"There's someones...someones I want you to meet!" His voice raised a pitch.

"Huh?"

"C'mon, 'Manda! C'mon!" He tugged, but she dug in her heels as she noticed a salon.

An actual salon. Hooray for small wonders!

She stopped, reading the front of the display window from across the street. *Manes on Main. Manicures. Pedicures. Colors. Perms.*

She sighed in relief.

The front door opened with a jingle of bells. A tall, thin man in his early thirties stepped out on the stoop to light a cigarette. He had beautiful, lush blond hair and high cheekbones. He was much too pretty for a man. He gave her a blinding white smile when he noticed them staring like a couple of idiots.

Greg suddenly released her hand and started to twist his together in a constant wringing motion. Amanda was quickly learning that he did that whenever he was stressed or excited.

"That's Teddy—Theo's name for short. Mama says he's gay. I don't know what that means." Amanda felt a flush rise from her throat. Greg continued on. "He cuts hair. But Mama won't let Teddy cut my hair. Why do people call him Teddy when his name is Theo?"

Amanda gave Teddy-Theo a crooked smile. She really wanted to hide, but there was nothing but a municipal waste can nearby. *That* wouldn't have been too obvious. So instead she dumped her empty latte cup in it and got a better grip on the shopping bag, just in case Greg took off dragging her down the middle of Main Street without a warning.

"Well, Greg, just like people call me Mandy sometimes or like you call me 'Manda. It's a nickname."

"What's a nick...nickname?"

"Like me calling you Greg instead of your full name of Gregory."

"Like you call me Bud?"

"Exactly. That's very good, Greg."

He puffed out his chest. "My name is Gregory Martin Barber."

"I know. Let's go say hello to Teddy." She caught him at the elbow, nudging him forward.

Greg pulled back, his eyes widening. "No! Mama says I can't talk to strangers."

"Greg, he's not a stranger; you know who he is."

"But...but, Mama says he's strange."

"Greg..." Amanda paused, then let out a frustrated sigh. "Never mind."

Amanda grabbed Greg's arm and hauled him across the street to the entrance of the salon.

"Hello."

Teddy parted his lips, then casually blew a stream of smoke up and away from them. "Hello."

"I'm so sorry."

"Don't apologize. This is a small town; I'm used to it. And I know it's not Greg's fault." Teddy smiled at Greg. "Hello, Greg."

Greg kept his eyes downcast, staring at his feet as he dug the toe of his sneaker into the concrete.

"Say hello, Greg," Amanda prompted. She nudged his back. When he still didn't answer, she nudged harder.

"Hello," he finally mumbled without lifting his head.

Teddy brought his attention back to Amanda.

"You're Amanda Barber."

"Yes, how did you know?"

Teddy laughed. "Welcome to Small Town America."

Not amused, Amanda asked, "So are you Theo, Teddy, Theodore or what?"

"My friends call me Teddy, others call me..." He glanced at Greg. "Well, you can imagine."

By the time Amanda had finished talking with Teddy, Greg had all but forgotten whom he wanted Amanda to meet. He was tired; so was she. So they agreed to head back to the house.

As they turned a corner on their walk back to the parking lot, Amanda noticed a man in a blue uniform by her car. He looked like a cop. She stopped dead in her tracks. He *was* a cop! One that was totally engrossed in writing on a silver metal clipboard.

And putting a copy of whatever it was under *her* windshield wiper. *Shit!*

She took off running, leaving Greg behind her screaming, "There's the someones I want you to see!"

Out of breath she skidded to a halt in front of the uniformed officer, pushing the hair out of her face.

He had a typical cop's haircut—the dark hair was nothing more than an extremely short crew cut. His crystal-blue eyes bored into her with a look of *caution: she may be crazy.* His square jaw tensed as if waiting for a confrontation. And Amanda didn't want to disappoint him.

"Hey, you can't do that!" Amanda dropped the bag of dog toys to yank her low-cut jeans back up since they had slipped dangerously lower as she ran. The last thing she needed was another citation for indecent exposure.

"Let me guess, this is your car?" His not so subtle sarcasm irritated her. Before she could give him a real piece of her mind, Greg had caught up.

"Max...Max...look what we buy Chaos!"

The officer's eyes softened and his jaw relaxed as he became aware of Greg.

"Hey, Greg. What are you doing out here by yourself?"

Amanda bristled. "He's not by himself. He's with me."

"Max! Max...this is my sister, 'Manda." Greg snagged the bag of dog toys from the ground and opened it wide to give Max a view inside. "See what we gots Chaos?"

To Greg's delight, Max took a good look in the bag, telling Greg how cool the toys were. While the officer was occupied with her brother, Amanda went over and ripped the yellow citation out from under the wiper. She scanned it.

"What? Why am I getting a parking ticket? This is free parking!"

He looked up slowly, raising one eyebrow. "Read the sign."

"Look, Officer..." She leaned in, reading his shiny name tag. "Bryson. I read the sign. It says *free parking*." She jammed her hands on her hips with emphasis.

She shouldn't have done that. Her action drew his frosty blue eyes down to the exposed skin between her low-riding waistline and the baby tee she wore. She jerked the edges of her jacket closed.

"It says free *two-hour* parking."

Amanda opened her mouth to argue, but as she read the sign again, it formed into an O. Her lips flattened shut. With a flourish she raised her arm and pulled back the sleeve of her leather coat, glancing at the delicate gold Bulova watch that dangled around her wrist.

The watch was one of many gifts her mother had given her to cover her maternal guilt. One ten. She had parked the car in the lot a little before eleven.

"You're kidding me right?" She gaped at him in disbelief. He casually lifted a shoulder in answer. "Fifteen minutes over and I'm getting a"—she looked at the now crumpled ticket in her hand — "twenty-five-dollar fine? Give me a break!"

Apparently he was used to dealing with angry citizens, as she didn't faze him. Amanda dug out the car keys and pushed the Unlock button on the car remote. Then she popped the trunk, threw in the bag of dog toys, and gave it a satisfying slam shut.

"I guess since there's no crime in this Hicksville of a town, you have nothing better to do than to harass law-abiding citizens. What do you do? Sit around with a stopwatch just waiting for someone to go over the time limit? Do those tickets pay your salary? Do you have a quota? Huh?"

Officer Bryson quietly watched her, feet planted shoulder-width apart. He remained calm and completely disturbing. His refusal to argue infuriated her further.

"Greg, get in the car. And don't forget your seatbelt. I don't need Officer Brightless here giving me another ticket."

She was relieved that Greg didn't resist, and once he was settled in the passenger seat, Amanda slammed the door shut. She gave the officer a final glare.

"How old are you?" The officer's voice was soft and low, and the question was so unexpected that she answered automatically.

"Twenty-eight." She then cursed herself for answering.

With deliberate care, he tucked his pen in his shirt pocket. "Really?" His gaze raked her body; then he tilted his head in contemplation. "Because the way you're acting, I'd have thought you were twelve."

Twelve? What a jerk!

"And from what I hear, Amanda, you are now responsible for your brother. I'd say you have some fast growing up to do."

Amanda moved around to the driver's side before she did something stupid and ended up in cuffs, stuffed in the back of his car, and—not to mention—being charged with assault on a police officer.

She raised her thumb up. "First, it's Ms. Barber to you." She raised her index finger next. "Second, nobody asked you." She narrowed her eyes and then lifted her middle finger up by itself. "And, third, it's none of your damn business."

Make that being charged with aggravated assault. With a side of disorderly conduct.

He dropped his head, and his body jerked. Was he laughing at her? After a second, he faced her again. "Just keep it that way. Keep yourself out of trouble, *Ms. Barber*. And don't be dragging Greg into any either. Or a twenty-five-dollar citation will be the least of your worries."

Amanda got in the car and locked the doors. She didn't like his warning...his threat. And she didn't like him.

Officer Max Bryson. One name she'd never forget.

· · ·

MAX SHOOK his head and let out a slow breath as he watched the little red car pull away with a squeal of tires. His pulse thumped so fiercely that he thought his veins would pop. He'd bet the one at his temple was visibly throbbing right now. He struggled to keep himself looking cool on the outside, while he didn't feel so composed on the inside. He usually didn't let disgruntled citizens get him riled up, especially since he knew most of them. He was used to dealing with people unhappy with their situations, whether their own fault or not.

What caught him off guard was his body's unexpected reaction to her. It had been quite a while since he'd felt an attraction that strong to someone. Especially that powerful. And never that instant. He ran a hand over his damp brow. What a little spitfire. When Max had heard that Greg's older sister was coming to town to take care of the boy, he hadn't given it another thought. He actually didn't think she'd show up. He really thought Greg would end up being stuck in a group home.

All he had heard about her around town was that *Ms.* Amanda Barber hadn't shown up for her father's funeral a couple of years ago. Of course, being a small, tight-knit community, that didn't go unnoticed and had been on everyone's lips for at least a month. Well, that was until the next big town "news" came along —which just happened to be Max's brother's reserve unit going off to the Middle East.

But the girl had come through; she had actually shown up to take responsibility for her sibling. Or half-sibling.

Either way, she sure didn't look like she could handle someone like Greg. Not that you could judge a book by its cover —as nice a cover as it was. Max hoped she proved him wrong.

He had a feeling he'd be running into her again.

Max smiled and wandered back to his patrol car. Yes, he was certain he'd be seeing her again. Soon.

And preferably under different circumstances.

Chapter Three

HE WAS WEARING that damn dark blue uniform again. But this time the shirt was unbuttoned, hanging open to show the white T-shirt he had on underneath it.

He unfastened his black leather belt and slowly slipped it out of the belt loops. Like he was stripping. He was teasing her! He dropped it to the floor. He removed the uniform shirt and flung it across the room. The T-shirt underneath hugged his skin, giving her a preview of what was underneath it.

He was getting undressed way too slow.

With a yank, the T-shirt was gone too. She waited for him to grab the front of his pants and pull, like an exotic dancer would with Velcro pants. One tug and *whoosh*! Nothing but leopard-print thong on.

But she was disappointed when that didn't happen; he just sat on the corner of the bed and removed his black boots. Like a normal person. He turned to look at her.

She was naked and waiting on the bed. Her nipples hardened under his gaze, and she ran her fingers over them, circling. They were sensitive and begging for his touch. His mouth. His tongue.

She bet he knew just what to do with that tongue.

He stood, the mattress evening out from the lack of his weight. He faced her with a hungry look. It was like he wanted to eat her.

Well, if he did, she wasn't going to complain. In fact, she would be quite accommodating.

She bent her knees and let them fall open, giving him a view that she hoped he'd never forget.

She sucked on her finger just enough to wet it, then stroked herself. She spread her lips, showing him just how much she wanted him. She was ready.

"Officer, I've been a bad girl." She pouted.

"Have you now? What have you done?"

He unfastened his pants and slid them down, kicking them out of the way, his eyes never leaving her face.

Damn. He was hung.

Her heart beat a little faster.

"Things I can't even tell you about..."

"Do I need to punish you?"

She nodded her head. The throbbing inside her made her toes clench.

He sat on the edge of the bed again, but leaned over to pick something off the floor.

He came back up with metal handcuffs hanging from his right hand.

A breathless "yes" escaped her.

He climbed over her to straddle her with his long legs. "Are you going to cooperate?"

Amanda's voice caught, and she could only nod.

"So, you regret being a bad girl?"

She nodded again, her heart pounding in her throat.

"Put your hands above your head."

She shimmied down a bit and reached her hands back until

they brushed the headboard. "You're not going to hurt me, are you, Officer?"

"I would never hurt you, you naughty girl. I'm here to protect and serve."

The cuffs were cold as he tightened them around her wrists; they were threaded through one of the bars on her headboard so she couldn't escape.

Not that she'd be a flight risk. She wasn't planning on going anywhere.

"How—" She swallowed hard. "How are you going to serve me?"

"I can't tell you. I need to show you."

His finger stroked lightly down her neck. She shivered; her nipples perked to the point of pain. That didn't go unnoticed. He was a good officer, so observant. He didn't miss a thing. She smiled.

Large hands, lightly dusted with dark hair, moved their way down her shoulders to her breasts. She arched her back in anticipation. She wasn't disappointed. His strong fingers plucked at her. Pulled. Twisted. Just how she wanted. Just how she liked it.

She groaned and thrashed her legs, making the cuffs clank against the headboard.

Sliding a hand down to her belly, he held her still. He shifted until he was settled in between her legs.

He stroked the soft, baby skin of her outer pussy with his fingers, then his tongue.

"You're so soft and smooth," he whispered, dipping a finger inside her. Then a second one. "You are so wet."

He kissed her swollen clit and then sucked it hard, making her cry out and thrash around.

Going to his knees, he held his hard length. She wanted him inside her. Now!

"Are you ready for me?" He stroked his cock slowly. Running

his thumb between her lips, he collected some of her wetness, then rubbed it over the head of his cock. "I'm ready for you. Can you see how hard I am?"

Amanda barely nodded her head. She could no longer speak.

He placed the crown of his cock right at her opening and shifted his weight over her.

Just as he was starting to slide into her, to fill her, Amanda's eyes popped open.

She was breathing hard, a drop of sweat rolling down her forehead. The sweat was real. Her dream was not.

Her pussy was throbbing but empty. *Damn.*

Something woke her up before she could finish her wet dream. She tried to slow her breathing so she could hear what it was.

Was someone at the front door? And why wouldn't they stop that loud, insistent rapping?

She peeked at the alarm clock: 6:30.

With a groan, she threw the covers over her head. Who in their right mind was up at this hour in the morning? Sunday morning at that. Wasn't it supposed to be a "day of rest?"

If she ignored whoever it was, they might go away and she could go back to her dream. Finish what she started.

The rapping turned into a ringing of the doorbell. Then it alternated. Rap, ring. Rap, ring.

It was enough to wake up the freaking dead. Releasing a growl, she tossed the covers back and got up. The cold air hitting her heated skin made her gasp.

She glanced over at the thermometer that clung outside her bedroom window: 62 degrees. *Ugh.*

She jammed a thick pair of socks onto her feet and snagged a robe, pulling it over her pajamas as she trudged down the hall. She peered into Greg's room as she passed.

Still sleeping. How could he sleep through that racket?

Why wouldn't whoever it was just go away?

When she reached the front door, Chaos was sitting attentively in front of it staring, his bushy tail slowly sweeping the floor, back and forth. Some guard dog; he hadn't even barked.

Well, whoever it was, she was going to give them hell.

She brushed Chaos aside with her foot and flung the door open.

"What!" She stopped and frowned. "Oh...hello."

"About time you got yourself out of bed."

A gray-haired, heavyset woman in her late sixties stood in front of her. She wore a multicolored housedress—the kind with the zipper down the front—black knee-high socks, and tan orthopedic shoes. Amanda winced at the ghastly fashion faux pas.

The woman's jowls jostled as she shoved a plate heaped with cookies at Amanda.

"Here, they're peanut butter. Greg likes them." She gave Chaos the evil eye. "I don't know why Dolores ever bought him that damn noisy dog."

As if mocking her, the *quiet* Chaos thumped his tail blissfully against the floor in response. Damn dog.

"I'm Amanda."

"I know. I live next door. Dolores told me all about you."

Great. "And you are?"

"Mrs. Myers." The older woman eyed Amanda up and down. "*Hmph.* I told Dolores a girl that doesn't even care enough to come home for her father's funeral doesn't have enough sense to take care of that poor boy." She scowled. "I'm sure you'll prove me right."

Amanda's grip tightened on the cookie plate as she glared at the miserable old bitch before her.

She took a deep breath before saying sweetly, "Well, I appreciate you welcoming me into the neighborhood, Mrs. Myers, especially so bright and early on this fine Sunday morning. I'm sure we'll become great friends."

Mrs. Myers raised a finger and shook it in Amanda's face, causing her to take a small step back. "I'll be watching you, young lady. You better take good care of that boy. And make sure I get that plate back."

With another *hmph* she turned and waddled back to her house.

"Nice meeting you," Amanda called out and slammed the front door shut.

She gave the dog a look. "I give you permission to bite her if she ever steps on this property again."

She considered the cookies in her hand. She peeled the plastic wrap back and dropped the plate to the floor. "There you go, Chaos. Enjoy."

She smiled as the dog gobbled up a couple of the cookies, his tail wagging enthusiastically. Then as he was licking a couple more, she stopped him. The last thing she needed was the dog getting sick. She certainly didn't want to clean up dog puke. Maybe she'd give them to Chaos one at a time. Like homemade dog treats.

She plucked the plate from underneath him and smoothed the wrap back over the surviving cookies. She'd have to hide them so Greg wouldn't eat the peanut butter cookies with the dog saliva icing.

SHE HEARD THE *WOOP, woop* of the siren behind her. Amanda slammed her hand on the steering wheel; she had almost made it home.

All she had wanted to do was to go to the Super Walmart at the edge of town, pick up a few groceries and some necessities, then get home. It should have been that simple. It *could* have been that simple.

Three more blocks and she would have made it. She had even waited until dark to go.

She put on the turn signal and, with a huff, pulled over to the curb. A bright spotlight pinned her in the car from behind. She powered down the window, and tapped her nails with an impatient rhythm on the frame.

"What the hell!" Officer Bryson's head filled up the car window, and a Maglite was pointed directly at her, blinding her. "Didn't I tell you not to get into trouble?"

"What?" she asked with feigned innocence. She impatiently pushed the flashlight out of her face.

"You are driving around town without a registration plate on your vehicle."

"Oh, it's missing?" She had removed the GREGSMOM plate from the sedan the other day. She tried to change the subject. "Are you the only cop in this town?"

"Fortunately for you, no. There are also my brothers Matt and Marc, to name a couple. I seemed to be the fortunate one to keep dealing with you, though. The way you're going, you'll meet them all soon enough."

"So your whole family is the police department?" At least send one of his other brothers. They can't all be barbarians like this one. "I guess I'll have to get another plate for the car."

"What happened to the old one?"

The one that she had tossed into the garbage? She wondered if that was a crime. "Uh...it was stolen?"

"We'll have to report it stolen then. And you'll have to notify PennDOT."

"Maybe it fell off."

He eyed her suspiciously. The tick in his jaw was growing by the minute. "Which was it?" he prodded. "Amanda, was it stolen or lost?"

Why couldn't he let this go? Why not just write her another stinking ticket and send her on her way? Every time she looked up at him, she was reminded of her dream. Why the hell would she pick someone so controlling to be in her wet dream? "I don't know."

"What?"

She raised her voice and repeated, "I don't know!"

"Well, I'll report it stolen then. I'm sure if someone around here took it," he lifted a brow, "then we will surely notice a vehicle with the plate GREGSMOM on it."

Amanda choked back a groan. "Yes, it shouldn't be too hard to miss."

"Well, when you get home, Amanda—*Ms. Barber*—make sure you take a *good* look around to see if it fell off. I suggest checking in the garage. If you find it, give us a call."

Amanda's felt the heat crawling up her neck. "I'll do that."

"I'll let you go this time. But if I catch you driving without a plate again, I'm towing your car."

How sweet.

"I'll follow you home."

How embarrassing, she thought as the black-and-white cruiser followed her up the street to the house.

How embarrassing Mrs. Myers, the next-door nosy neighbor just happened to be out on her porch. At nighttime. With only a bare yellow bulb lighting up her stocky figure, hands on her hips in clear disapproval.

As she pulled into the paved driveway, the cruiser continued on down the street. She stopped the vehicle and stared back at Mrs. Myers. The woman didn't like her. It was mutual.

Great. Now she was dealing with a meddling cop *and* a meddling neighbor. What was next?

SHE SHOULD HAVE NEVER ASKED herself that question. She appeared to be stuck in the midst of Murphy's Law.

The next morning, she went to wake up Greg, to get him ready for adult day care. His bed was empty.

She tried not to panic. She checked the bathroom. Empty. She whistled for Chaos. No response.

She ran down the stairs and out into the backyard. Empty.

She checked the car in the garage. It sat there empty.

Now she could panic.

She grabbed a jacket and a pair of sneakers, pulling them on as she went, and rushed out the front door.

Only to be brought up short.

A police car pulled up in the driveway. She relaxed somewhat when she spotted Chaos and Greg in the backseat.

She grimaced as she heard a *tsk tsk* from the direction of the porch next door. She ignored the old busybody.

At least it wasn't Officer Bryson driving the cruiser. Last thing she needed right now was another lecture from that man. Anyway, she didn't *think* it was him. As the car rolled to a stop, she rushed forward to open the back passenger-side door.

Fortunately, her brother was in one piece. "Greg! Where were you? You scared me!"

She gave him a big hug and brushed a lone lock out of his eyes.

The disturbingly familiar-looking police officer unfolded himself from the driver's seat. "Ma'am. I'm Officer Bryson. I mean, Marc Bryson." He gave her a half smile as he said, "I've heard you've already met my brother Max."

They were eerily similar. The same closely cropped dark hair, ice-blue eyes, strong square jaw, and deep tan, like they both spent a lot of time outdoors. This one had quite a few less creases around the eyes, though. And he didn't look so disapproving. Or barbarian.

"What happened?"

He tilted a head toward the busybody and lowered his voice. "Mrs. Myers called and said she saw Greg running away from home."

"What?"

Greg piped in at that moment. "I wasn't runnin' away! I wasn't, 'Manda."

"We found him down on Fifth Street."

"Fifth Street! Holy shit." Amanda grimaced, realizing she'd just cursed in front of a police officer on duty. She turned to Greg and took his shoulders, giving him a little shake. "What were you doing on Fifth Street?"

"Looking for Mama."

His sullen answer tore at her heart. She didn't know what to say, how to respond.

"Ma'am..."

"Amanda," she corrected him. She was not ready for that old-lady title yet. Save it for Mrs. Busybody.

"Amanda..." With a hand on her back, he steered her away from Greg so they could talk privately. He kept his voice low as he continued, "His mother's church is on Fifth."

Amanda shook her head. She didn't understand.

He cleared his throat. "That's where her service was."

Her service... Ah! What an idiot she was. The people in this town must think her heartless. No wonder Mrs. Busybody didn't like her. Amanda had never visited. She never even came back for her father's funeral. Or her stepmother's.

No wonder Officer Max Bryson thought her immature and selfish. She looked up at his brother; nothing but pity showed in his blue eyes. Right now she felt so low that she'd rather have had Max's disapproval staring down at her. Punishing her.

She deserved it.

As if in slow motion, she turned away and sank down on the concrete front stoop. She looked at her brother, who was helpless in this world. She was all he had.

Greg remained standing next to the black-and-white car with an abnormal calmness, not his excitable self. Chaos sat at his feet obediently—also unnaturally still.

She studied the dog. Chaos didn't know his master was different. Chaos didn't care.

She was so in over her head. But she was determined not to drown.

———

AMANDA GLANCED OVER AT GREG, who was coloring with crayons...only he didn't have a coloring book. He was immersed in decorating the kitchen table. Amanda closed her eyes and sighed.

She had insisted Greg stay home from day care and had spent half the morning trying to explain why his mother wasn't still waiting for him at the Fifth Street church. He had heard everything she had to say, but hadn't really *listened*.

And Amanda was tired of trying to explain. Both of them ended up extremely agitated for most of the day. Even Chaos had gone out his doggy door to escape the tension.

Maybe she just needed to get Greg away from this place.

"Bud, how about moving to the big city?"

Without even looking up, he mumbled, "No."

Amanda moved around the table to stand next to his seat. She stroked her fingers over his hair. "Maybe you could meet new friends."

"No."

"Why? Greg, don't you want lots of friends and lots of things to do?"

"Don't wanna leave."

"Why?"

"Mama may come back."

"Greg..." Amanda reached out and grabbed Greg's hands with hers, ceasing their senseless movement. "Greg, your mama isn't coming back."

"Yes, she might."

"Did Daddy?"

Greg's hands tensed against hers, his fingers clench tight. "No... no... Daddy's gone for good. Mama says so."

"Yes, and your mama is with our daddy."

"No. She's coming back."

"No, Greg..."

"Yes, she said she'd never leave me."

"I'm sure she did."

"She said so!" He jerked away and stared down at the broken crayons in his hands. "Oh, my crayons are broke. Mama's gonna be mad!"

Amanda sank into a chair at the table. "No, she won't."

"'Manda, stop it! Stop it! Mama said..."

"Greg, your mama said a lot of things, but..."

Greg suddenly pushed away from the table, causing his chair to flip backward with a crash. He towered over Amanda, his face flushed, a piece of spittle caught in the corner of his mouth. "SHUT UP!"

Amanda had to cover her ears to protect them from his high-pitched shriek. His fists were clenched and his eyes wild. For the first time, Amanda felt a spark of fear. She might have pushed him too far.

Max Bryson stepped into the kitchen. A fleeting thought of how he had gotten into the house crossed her mind. He approached Greg, put his hands on the younger man's shoulders, and gave them a slight squeeze. "Hey, pal, what's going on?"

The tension notably lessened in Greg's body. For that she was grateful. Why Max was in her house was another thing. She realized then that she had been holding her breath; she released it in a rush.

"Max! 'Manda wants to take me away!"

Heat rose from her neck into her cheeks when Max gave her a quick glance. He frowned. "She does?"

"Yeah, she wants me to go...to the big city an'...an'...meet new people an' get new things."

"She does? And you don't want to go? Well, we will have to convince her that you want to stay."

Amanda hissed, "Like it's any of your business." She got up and grabbed the furniture polish from under the sink. She began to scrub at the crayon marks on the kitchen table with a rag.

The more she thought about Max putting his nose in their business, the harder she scrubbed. She tuned out their conversation and concentrated on removing the colored wax from the wood's finish. When she was done, she looked up and realized it was quiet.

Greg had left the room, and Max was leaning back against the center island, arms and feet crossed. He was watching her intently.

"Do you have nothing better to do? Like go fight crime? Or write a little old lady a citation for jaywalking? Did you lose your parking-lot stopwatch?"

The corner of his lip curled up. "You should be fined for having such a cute ass. Just watching you wiggling it back and forth like that as you scrubbed gave me a—"

He stopped abruptly, as if he had just realized he had said his thoughts out loud. The surprise on his face was quickly schooled to a blank expression.

As she finished his thought, Amanda's gaze flew downward.

She turned to gather Greg's broken crayons and threw them into an old coffee can, closing the lid with a snap. She could finally look up at Max without blushing. "Again...why are you here? And most importantly, how did you get in?"

"Well, I got in through your front door. It wasn't locked."

"Do you normally just barge into people's homes?"

"No, only in emergencies. I heard the yelling and thought there might be one."

Amanda snorted. She stilled, her eyes narrowed. "Did that busybody call you?"

"Who?"

"Never mind. What do you want?"

"I heard what happened this morning and wanted to check up on you and Greg."

Ah.

"My brother said you were pretty distressed."

"Of course I was. Do you think I don't care about my brother?"

"I didn't say that."

"You didn't have to."

"Look, this is a small town. Everybody knows everything. Or at least thinks they know everything. That's just the way it is. Maybe down in—Miami, is it?—it's no big deal that a daughter doesn't come home for a funeral, but up here... Well, people talk."

"That's because there's nothing to do except gossip and talk about things people don't know anything about."

"Maybe so."

"No maybes about it. Oh, and give out unfair citations. Can't forget that one!"

"You're lucky I didn't give you one the other day when your registration plate got *lost*."

Out of nowhere it hit Amanda that *this* was Max Bryson.

Not Officer Max Bryson. He wasn't in uniform. She was suddenly taken aback on how handsome he looked. Without the uniform he looked less...barbaric? Militant. Less patronizing.

His jeans fit him quite nicely, while his worn flannel shirt with the rolled-up sleeves looked soft against the deep tan of his forearms. A deep blue T-shirt peeked out from the V of the tucked in flannel. She couldn't imagine him with his hair any longer than it was. The severe haircut fit him. Her pulse quickened.

He was a true *man*. Masculine. Mature.

She wondered if he would look as naked in real life as he did in her dream. She licked her lips.

"Don't." His voice was low and gruff, clearly a warning.

Amanda closed her eyes and tried to speak.

She cleared her throat and tried again. "I appreciate your concern, but I think you'd better leave." Her eyes opened, and she met his, the fiery blue ice making her breath catch. "I see you're off duty, and I'm sure you have better things to do with your time."

He straightened up, uncrossing his legs and arms. "You're right." He stepped close to her, hesitated just for a second. Just long enough for Amanda to feel the searing heat of his body. Goosebumps broke out over her skin. He brushed by with some parting words. "Stay out of trouble."

As she watched him take long strides out of the kitchen, she caught herself on the counter before her knees collapsed.

AFTER SAYING goodbye to Greg on his way out, Max stepped out of the house and took a deep breath of the cool fall air. He needed to clear his head. Marc had tried to warn him not to go over to check up on her, but Max hadn't agreed. He thought it was the perfect opportunity to see Amanda on a non-police matter. Hopefully on more pleasant terms.

Unfortunately, it hadn't turned out that way. As he had arrived, he had heard Greg's out-of-control yelling, and he had rushed in to see Amanda in way over her head. As he had previously feared. He sighed.

What he had hoped to be a nice little neighborly visit turned wrong. He frowned and walked over to his truck. Hopping in, he sat in the cab, staring at the little house in front of him.

Max had noticed when Amanda's expressive gaze had changed. One second she was being a major bitch, the next she was checking him out with those sizzling eyes. *Phew.* Again he was surprised at the quick response from his body. He was losing control.

He strapped the seat belt across his torso.

He had to meet up with her again. Next time it would be better without conflict brewing. Maybe he should ask her out for coffee.

Hell, he'd make it a beer instead. She needed to loosen up.

MAX KNOCKED on Amanda's door. No answer. He knocked again. He tried the knob. It was locked, unlike last time he was there.

He heard a faint, "Who is it?"

"Ma'am? It's Officer Bryson, ma'am. Please open the door."

"Why? What's going on?"

"It's police business, ma'am."

The door swung open, giving him an unobstructed view of Amanda in the sexiest teddy he'd ever seen.

"Will you stop calling me ma'am? I'm not that old. And hurry up and come in; it's chilly out there."

It sure was. Her nipples perked underneath the silky fabric—the black lacy fabric that barely covered her full breasts. He swore he could see the rosy color of her nipples.

She closed the door behind him and turned to face him.

"Is this going to be quick, Officer?"

"Oh, I can make it quick." Then he grimaced when he realized what he'd said. *Damn it!*

"What was so important that you had to wake me out of bed?"

"Ma'am... Amanda, you never paid your parking ticket. I have a warrant for your arrest."

"What? A warrant? Let me see it."

Max checked his pockets and couldn't find the warrant. He cleared his throat. "Well, I can't find it right this second. But it's a bench warrant."

"Well, can I pay you now?" She took a step closer.

Why was she wearing that sexy outfit? This was supposed to be police business. He wasn't able to concentrate on the matter at hand. This wasn't like him.

"Yes, I'll take payment."

"Cash, check, or...?"

"Or?"

She moved another step forward and was now inches from him. Her nipples were clearly visible through that lace.

"Or...how about this?" She closed the few inches between them, stood on her tiptoes, and brushed his lips with hers.

She leaned back just enough for him to say, "That's not sufficient."

She kissed him again, this time grabbing his waist for balance, holding her lips against his a little longer. When she pulled back, he just shook his head.

"No? Well, how about this?" She smashed her lips to his and

plundered his mouth with her tongue, exploring every corner until he groaned.

Her hand reached down and slipped into the waistband of his jeans, just enough to grab the hem of his T-shirt, then rip it over his head, tossing it to the floor. She leaned in and rubbed her breasts against his chest. The feel of the silky fabric and her hard nipples almost made him pick her up and throw her onto the couch.

Instead, she grabbed the waistband of his jeans again and tugged him over to the couch.

Damn, she wanted all the control.

"Take your pants off."

After kicking off his boots, he did just that. His cock was hard and ready, and his balls were tight. The blood was surging through his body, his heart pumping rapidly.

Amanda gave him a shove, and he landed on the couch, giving him a complete view of her in that black teddy. Besides the lace that barely concealed her breasts, solid black fabric draped down to her hips. Just long enough that he couldn't tell if she had panties on.

His gaze roamed her legs from the tops of her thighs down to her toes, appreciating every curve that she had. Her inner thigh, her knees, her calves.

"C'mere," he said, his voice so gravelly that he didn't sound like himself. He reached out a hand, and she took it. He drew her into him, and she was suddenly straddling him. His cock was caught between her bare pussy—well, there was the answer—and his lap. He was right there. Right there! It wouldn't take much but a minor shift.

She leaned into him and captured his lips again, moaning as their tongues tangled and explored. Her fingers tweaked his nipples, making him jerk a little but not enough to lose the touch of their kiss.

He broke free so he could push down the spaghetti straps of her teddy, releasing her breasts. They were perfect and beautiful. He buried his face between them, kissing her flushed skin. He sucked one nipple while he teased the other with his fingers, twisting just enough to make her cry out, sink harder in his lap, and grind against him.

His cock twitched against her heat, feeling her wetness. He brushed his teeth over the other nipple, reaching his thumb down in between them to find her clit. She bucked against him like a wild horse. And with a little lift and tilt of her hips, she captured his cock. A long, low moan escaped her as she lowered herself slowly, ever so slowly, until she had him completely enveloped inside her. Her inner muscles squeezed him as she rode him, easy at first, then she picked up the pace. His head fell against the couch as she controlled the movement. Up, down, circling. Almost letting him go, then quickly swallowing him again.

Her hips shifted and tilted as she reached back to stroke his balls, then squeeze them. He almost lost it right there. He tried to slow his breathing, but she was wreaking havoc on his control.

He wanted this to last. But between her little whimpers and her clenching pussy, he was going to lose it.

And when she cried out, "I'm coming!" he lost it.

His cock throbbed as he spilled into her, his release mixing with hers...

He rolled over and woke up.

He dragged a hand over his stomach. Sticky. It was only a dream. A freaking teenage-like wet dream. *Fuuuuuuuuck.*

That damn woman has gotten under his skin.

Chapter Four

SHE SHOULD HAVE COME up with the idea sooner. Using her reflection in the glass door, Amanda made sure her hair was in place and her clothes in proper order before pushing the door open with one hand. The other was occupied with balancing the plate of Mrs. Busybody's peanut butter cookies.

She had wanted to do something nice for Officer Marc Bryson. And when she found the plate of cookies in the back of the cabinet where she had hidden them, the thought came to mind. He would never know that she didn't make them herself. Or that the dog licked them...

Her high-heeled boots tapped along the tiled floor as she entered the police station. An American flag occupied one corner with the Commonwealth of Pennsylvania flag parked right next to it. On the walls were framed pictures of men in uniform. She couldn't tell if they were current or former officers, but clearly not one was a woman. Figures. A small town such as this probably didn't recognize equal rights. It was like the Dark Ages.

She thought she spotted one of the Brysons' pictures up

there, but she wasn't sure and before she could step closer to read the brass plate underneath it, she was interrupted.

"Can I help you?"

She stepped up to the counter and smiled at the redheaded officer. A dusting of freckles crossed his nose and cheeks. He wasn't much older than her. She read his name tag: Dunn.

"Hello, I'm just here to drop off some cookies for Officer Bryson."

"Oh, hold on. I think he's in the patrol room." Officer Dunn turned and bellowed toward the back. "Max, someone is here to see you."

Max! Amanda panicked. "No! No. That's not... I'm sorry, I meant Marc Bryson."

"Oh." He gave her a shrug like it was no big deal.

Too late.

Max came from out of a side room with his head down, busy snapping on the leather keepers that secured his duty belt to his narrow trouser belt. Amanda looked at the cluttered accessory and wondered what all the things hanging off it were for. The gun, of course, she recognized.

He looked up as he approached the front counter and froze. A flush flooded his face. Amanda's eyebrows knit together. She had never seen him embarrassed before. What did he have to be embarrassed about?

"*Ms. Barber.*"

"*Officer Bryson.*" She frowned. "Actually, I was here to see your brother."

The color left his face as quickly as it appeared. A dark eyebrow rose.

"I brought him some cookies to show my gratitude for bringing Greg home the other day."

She plunked the plate down on the counter. Both men eyed the cookies hungrily.

Typical men, she thought. Give them food or sex and they're happy. Pussy or cookies, just put them on a plate.

Max turned to Dunn. "Go take a break."

The other officer knocked Max's arm and said, "Save me a couple," before disappearing down a brightly lit hallway.

Max pulled the plastic wrap back and held a cookie up, inspecting it. Suddenly, Amanda felt horrified. She shouldn't have brought these cookies here. Chaos had slobbered on them. Maybe he could tell?

Ugh. Why didn't she even know how to bake something simple like cookies? She had wanted to thank Marc, not get him sick. Would it look suspicious if she suddenly knocked the cookie out of Max's hand and threw them all in the garbage?

"Are they poisoned?"

Without waiting for an answer, his straight, white teeth bit into the soft cookie. Amanda held her tongue until he finished chewing and swallowed.

"Yes," she said. And smiled.

He only hesitated for a second before finishing the rest of it off. "Well, they're good. I'll make sure you get the plate back."

She nodded and swept a hand toward his duty belt. "What's all the junk?"

The surprise showed on his face. She guessed that Max didn't believe she was actually interested.

She wasn't really, but for some silly reason, she wanted to make conversation. She couldn't imagine why since he was so aggravating.

Standing a little taller with unmistakable pride, he started on his right hip, placing a hand on each item as he went around the belt. "My weapon. It's a Glock .45. Expandable ASP baton. Two extra magazines. Holder for my Maglite."

"I thought I recognized that flashlight," she said with a little sarcasm. Just a little...

"Radio holder. Pepper spray. And these..." He popped open a black leather case and pulled out a set of shiny silver handcuffs, dangling them from one of his long fingers. "Are for bad little girls. Do you want to try them on for size?"

Damn, they were just like the ones in her dream. She closed her eyes, reliving it. Just for a second. Her eyes popped open when he cleared his throat.

"I have my own set, thank you very much." She gave him a wicked smirk. "They're pink and fuzzy."

She spun on her heels and tossed over her shoulder, "Enjoy the cookies. And stay out of my dreams."

As she walked away, leaving him speechless, the guilt came back to her again. She pushed the thought away. He deserved everything she gave him.

She heard him call out "What?" as she shoved the door open with a smile and walked out into the sunlight.

A little dog spit wasn't going to hurt anybody.

THE COOKIES WERE GONE, and the plate long returned to Mrs. Busybody's porch—in the middle of the night—as the end of October quickly blew into November. And as much as she hated —no, that was too strong—*disliked* Manning Grove, she had to admit to herself the fall foliage was beautiful.

The colder weather, she could do without, though.

Amanda had managed to stay out of trouble as Max had suggested on several occasions. Even better, she had actually managed to stay out of his way too. Occasionally she saw a black-and-white cruiser around town and wondered who was driving. Marc or Max or the other brother, whoever he was. She hadn't had the pleasure of meeting him yet. She preferred to stay out of the police department's attention. Even though one of their officers kept invading her dreams. But at least her dreams kept her warm at night.

She had redecorated the master bedroom to her liking, which made her feel a little more comfortable in the house.

In fact, she only left when she needed to pick up groceries or things they needed. She was trying to stay out of view from curious eyes. Especially Mrs. Busybody's.

She hadn't even left the house to meet with the lawyer. She had called Mr. Wells instead, just to let him know she'd be sticking around for a little while longer. And if anything changed, he'd be the first to know. He seemed satisfied with that for now.

Anyway, it wasn't like she could blend in easily; her sense of style alone made her stand out. But she refused to give up her fashionable wardrobe for boring housewife-type jeans and bulky sweatshirts with "cutesy" pictures on the front. Which seemed to be the fashion fad around here.

She had become close with Teddy. They spent hours talking like two girlfriends—on the phone or holed up in his shop. He really reminded her of home and some of the friends she'd left behind. Miami was a mecca of colorful people. She missed that.

The best part was that Amanda had finally set up her laptop and had cable—who in their right mind lived without cable nowadays?—installed in the house. So now she had Wi-Fi access. Finally, some connection to the real world.

As she was checking her neglected Facebook page, the familiar ding of her DM caught her attention. The chat window popped up on her screen.

She looked to see who'd sent her a message. *Carlos.*

Hey, baby, what r u doin, flashed before her.

Unfortunately, she hadn't blocked her status for others to see, so he knew she was online. The green little circle told him so.

Nothing, she typed, then hit the Enter key with a little more force than was necessary.

A second later: *I miss u.*

I bet, Amanda replied.

Do u 4give me?

No. She quickly blocked his profile and X-ed out of the window. That was that.

Until her cell phone rang thirty seconds later. She looked at the display. She recognized the number; the self-proclaimed "hot tamale" was now calling.

She swiped the screen. "What."

The heavy accent on the other end grated her nerves. "You shouldn't still be mad at me."

"Why not?"

He knew that she had every right to still be angry with him. Which was evident by the long pause. "I miss you, *pocita.*"

"You said that."

"I could come and visit."

Amanda laughed. Carlos in Manning Grove. Right.

It was almost as laughable as Amanda herself being in Manning Grove. She grimaced.

"I could bring *tu madre.*"

"No!"

"She misses you, as I do. Says it was a mistake that you left."

"That's her opinion. The only mistake I made was accepting you back for the second time after you slept with Rena." The cheating, lying *perro.*

"It won't happen again." He sounded like a little boy, and Amanda wondered what she'd ever seen in him. He had swept her off her feet with his hot Latino passion, but that was all it was. Nothing more. He was immature and still a little child. Sometimes he acted even younger than Greg.

"No, you're right, it won't. I'm done with you."

"You found another man."

"No." Well, maybe. Sort of. She found a man continually in

her thoughts. And her wet dreams. A man in a dark blue uniform. A proud, strong, amazingly annoying man. But a real man.

Not some little boy. She was finished with thirty-year-old little boys. Done with double-dealing dogs.

"No me llama otra vez." She heard a hurt sound on the other end before she cut off the call.

The phone rang again. Didn't she just tell him not to call?

She let the call go to voicemail and went back to catching up on her endless e-mails.

Within two minutes the phone rang again. Her mother.

She pushed the Power button, shutting the phone off. It was too coincidental. Her mother had probably put Carlos up to calling her. She thought Amanda would come running back to Carlos.

Well, she was wrong.

As much as she wanted to go back to Miami... Even if she could convince Greg, she would now have to wait. There was no way she wanted her mother to think she was coming back because of her. Or Carlos.

If she could survive this arctic tundra, she'd go back in spring. That gave her plenty of time to work on Greg.

An uneventful Thanksgiving came and went. The same lonely pumpkin that Amanda had purchased for Halloween served as the sole decoration for turkey day.

As the colorful leaves fell, barren trees were left in their wake. The winds picked up, causing Amanda to finally give in and dig out some of her stepmother's unattractive, bulky sweaters to wear. She had resisted for a while, but even with the heat on, she shivered in the house.

Passing a mirror in the upstairs' hall, she stopped and looked at herself in disgust. Apparently her stepmother had been a much larger woman, as the sweater she had pulled on fell to her knees and swallowed her whole. She looked like a big blob.

She had money accumulating in an account since she had hardly touched the trust except to pay for Greg's day care, food, and the utilities. She decided it was a good time to spend some of it.

She shucked the sweater. There was no way she was going out in public looking like that—she'd rather freeze to death. She made sure Greg was bundled up before packing him into the gray Buick, with the now nondescript license plate, and headed off to do some high-end shopping...at Kohl's. Besides Walmart, it was the only decent-sized store in the area.

A light dusting of snow covered the roads, and she ended up driving like an old woman. She was not used to driving in the stuff. Her knuckles white, she had to slowly unfold them from the steering wheel when she finally got to their destination. She realized she'd had her jaw clenched the entire time, and forced it to relax, rubbing away the stiffness.

Greg had teased her all the way, telling her she looked funny. She was too nervous to remove a hand from the steering wheel to turn up the stereo volume. She had wanted to drown out his deafening laughter.

When she had turned into the parking lot, the car's back end had slid a tiny bit, and she shrieked with fright. Greg had only enjoyed the ride and screamed, "Wheeeee!"

She had looked over at him in annoyance. It would serve him right if she made him drive home.

But she slowly relaxed as they strolled through the different departments. Greg was having a ball picking out items excitedly, spittle flying like crazy. He found the perfect outfit for Amanda: purple stockings, a lime spandex jumper and a pink turtleneck. Oh, and she couldn't forget the yellow beanie hat. Amanda handed it all to a clerk, apologizing. She felt bad that the young girl would have to put all the stuff back.

Instead, she went to the juniors department where the clothes were a bit more trendy and tried on some really cute tops along with some tight hip-riding jeans. On her umpteenth trip to the dressing room, she pulled on a snug, soft V-necked sweater in autumn gold and a deep forest-green corduroy mini. She tugged on some black leather knee-high boots and tromped out onto the sales floor amid the jungle of clothing racks.

"What do you think, Greg?"

Greg was not sitting on the vinyl seat where she'd left him right outside the dressing room. Instead he was talking with animation to none other than Officer Bryson. She sucked in a breath. He was in uniform with a dark navy cruiser jacket covering his wide shoulders. He carried a notepad in his hands.

And he was staring a hole right through her. Amanda's toes curled in the tight boots.

She went over, walking carefully in the stiff boots. She didn't need to trip and look like a dolt. "Is there a problem, Officer?"

Even though fully clothed, he made her feel naked as hell while raking his eyes over her. Warmth spread from her thighs.

His hand tightened on the notebook, and she noticed a quick clench and unclench of his jaw before speaking...a bit huskily. "Not at all." Max cleared the catch in his voice. "I was just here getting additional information on a previous incident."

"Oh. Sounds exciting."

"It's not. Greg was just telling me that you two had Thanksgiving alone."

Amanda shot a look at her brother. As always, it went unnoticed. Greg hopped from one foot to the other, nodding his head in agreement.

"We weren't alone," she said carefully. "We had each other."

"You don't have any other family you can spend the holidays with?"

Amanda frowned and muttered, "None that I want to spend it with."

"What?"

"None close by. I don't want to drag Greg down to Miami for just a few days." She added, "If I drag him down there, I want it to be permanent."

Amanda didn't miss his answering scowl. It wasn't any of his business anyway.

Max turned to Greg. "Want to spend Christmas with my family? We'll have a tree and presents, and we'll sing Christmas carols."

Greg squealed with delight, his arms swinging uncontrollably. It was a low blow not to ask her first in private before getting Greg's hopes up.

"And mistletoe..." He stared at her lips. She licked them instinctively.

He stepped forward. She stepped back. Their gazes locked.

Amanda finally broke free and looked at her brother. She couldn't disappoint him. She didn't want him to miss out on a fun holiday gathering. Even if it was with this disturbing man and his family. *His family.*

"Your wife won't mind?"

A deep rumbling started in Max's belly and worked its way up. "No. My wife won't mind."

He winked at Greg. Greg tried to wink back but ended up closing both of his eyes at the same time.

"Oh," she murmured, wondering why that question would be funny.

Max flipped open his notepad and scribbled down an address before ripping the page out of the book. "Here. Be there early enough to open presents." As she reached for it, he snagged it

50

back to scribble some more. "That's my cell. In case you get lost... or are late." He snapped the notepad closed and stuffed it into his back pocket. "But don't be late."

He was giving her an order!

His wandering gaze seared her from head to toes.

"And wear that outfit." With that he turned and strode away.

He was telling her what to wear? Whatever!

Chapter Five

Fuck him! Telling *her* what to wear.

Amanda studied herself in the long mirror, tugging slightly on her new corduroy skirt. She plucked a fuzzy off the gold sweater and wiggled her feet in the knee-high leather boots. She was wearing exactly what he wanted her to wear. With the addition of sheer black stockings. And some emerald jewelry she had discovered in her stepmother's jewelry box to accent her eyes.

She made sure Greg was dressed nicely before she loaded him and the presents she had wrapped—a little sloppily, but they were wrapped—into the horribly nondescript Buick.

As she drove through town, her stomach did a little dance.

She wanted to think she was just nervous about taking Greg to someone else's home. Hoping he didn't get out of control. But it wasn't that. She was actually learning to deal with her brother's swinging moods.

Instead, it was the thought of meeting Max's family. She assumed Marc would be there. And possibly the mysterious third brother Matt, supposedly another cop. She could only guess about the rest of the family. Max could have a wife and a herd of kids for all she knew. Though, if so, he was a dog for staring at her like he did.

Maybe he had taken pity on Greg and that was why he'd invited them. Not for her, but out of concern for her brother. As if she was incapable of providing a nice holiday for him.

Well, that was fine. She wanted to make her brother happy. And if being around a big family would be good for Greg, then so be it.

Still, she was sure she would feel like an outsider.

With a mental shake, Amanda reminded herself that everything wasn't about just her any longer.

Following Max's directions, she drove out of town and down a country road. Double-checking the number on the mailbox, she made a right into a long stone driveway. The painted wooden sign was hard to miss. Bryson's Christmas Tree Farm.

It certainly was. Dark green, beautifully groomed trees lined both sides of the driveway. A mini forest of pines blocked the view of any buildings until they got to a clearing.

An old, well-kept farmhouse appeared, flanked by several outbuildings. Some were small, old, and wooden, others large and metal. A couple tractors sat around the farmyard. In the driveway, a handful of trucks and SUVs were parked haphazardly. She felt out of place in the lone sedan. Apparently this was truck country.

Amanda had barely stopped the vehicle before Greg released his seatbelt, letting it fly. Amanda winced as the metal buckle smacked against the passenger-side window. At least it hadn't shattered. He flung the door open and ran up to the wraparound porch, shrieking with excitement.

Before she could even turn off the ignition, he was pounding on the front door. Greg disappeared inside as soon as it opened. Amanda climbed out of the car and stood staring, hands on her hips.

Now who was going to help her carry in all the packages?

Her answer came in the form of a tall, lean man bounding out of the house. He closed the gap between them quickly with his long strides.

His breath frosted the air as he spoke. "You must be Amanda."

She blinked at the image before her. This was exactly how Max would look in about twenty-five years. He could only be Max's father.

The well-built man reached out to give her a great big bear hug. Amanda yipped as she felt her ribs tighten.

"Pop! Pop! Put her down." With the same exact stride, Max came off the porch, following his father to the car.

When Pop Bryson dropped her to the ground, she grabbed Max's arm for support. Marc jogged down the front steps to join them. "Pop, are you molesting the guest?"

Amanda finally got her breath back and popped open the trunk. "Good. You guys can help me carry the presents in."

The three peered into the back of the car. It was jam-packed with brightly wrapped boxes.

Pop exclaimed, "You didn't need to bring us gifts, girl!"

Amanda blushed. "I didn't. They're for Greg. I wanted him to have gifts to open while everyone else is opening theirs."

"Don't you worry about that, girl. He'll have plenty of gifts. Now you just get yourself inside and warm up. Leave the heavy lifting to us men."

She did so gladly, even though none of the packages were heavy.

Her senses flooded as she stepped inside. The crisp scent of pine from the enormous fresh tree that sat in the front room blended nicely with the unmistakable smell of a turkey roasting in the oven. A soft glow of candles lit up the room. She looked at them with worry. She'd have to make sure Greg didn't knock them over, either burning himself with hot wax or torching the house down. She was shocked to realize that she was thinking like a mother with a small child—a child who was very curious and always into things.

A tinkle of laughter floated through the room, interrupting her thoughts. Amanda heard Greg's squeals mixed in. She followed the sound into the warm kitchen. She was relieved to see a handsome woman in her mid-fifties—not a beautiful young wife for Max—standing next to Greg. The woman was showing him how to baste the turkey. She was patiently holding his squirming hand steady, so he wouldn't squirt the hot juices anywhere but where they belonged.

"Okay, now step back and let me stick Tom Turkey back into the oven. He's got some time to go yet."

"Tom." Greg mimicked. "Yummy!" He spun and spotted Amanda. "'Manda! We's going to eat Tom."

"I see that. Tom looks good."

"Yummy! Yummy in my tummy." He rubbed his belly while doing a little jig, then laughed at his own goofiness.

The older woman stepped forward. After wiping her hands on a dish towel, she extended one. "I'm Mary Ann." She gave Amanda a warm smile. "And I'm sure you've met Ron."

Amanda rubbed her ribs. "Yes, he, Marc, and Max came out to greet me. They look a lot alike."

Mary Ann sighed. "The apple doesn't fall far from the tree. Or should I say bushel of apples? Cursed...Oops, I mean blessed with three boys. All look like Ron. Lucky for them, their father is a handsome man." She waved Amanda into a chair at the old plank-topped table, and she settled across from her. "Not only do they look like him. They all act like him. Stubborn. Possessive. Fiercely loyal. Did you know Ron is a retired cop? He worked on the same force they all work on now. For thirty years! Heck,

Ron's father was killed in the line of duty as a police officer. It's in the blood."

Amanda remembered the picture she had seen hanging at the police station. It made sense now. That had been Max's father.

"You haven't met Matt yet. He's home, at least for now. He's a jarhead. Again, they all were. Do you know what a jarhead is?"

Amanda didn't even attempt to answer; she just shook her head instead.

"A Marine. He's in the reserves, but originally he was sent over to fight in the Middle East. He's home for the holidays, but they'll be shipping him back overseas again in a couple weeks for who knows what. I just hope his tour is over soon and he comes home permanently. A mother can't help but worry."

"Mother!" An even younger version of Max, Ron, and Marc entered the kitchen. His very familiar eyes pinned Amanda to her seat. He looked to be about her own age.

"Well, can you blame me, Matt? I fretted while each of your brothers served. Why shouldn't I with you? Especially being over there in one of those godforsaken countries."

"Come on, Mom." Matt barked. "I'm only home for a short time. Let's not ruin it."

"Well, I wish you boys would just settle down and get married and give me some grandchildren."

A collective groan was heard from the other room. Amanda stifled a laugh. Mary Ann sniffed, throwing the dish towel on the table. She grabbed Greg by the hand. "Come on, my boy. Let's go open presents."

"Yes, presents. Lots of presents!" he crowed.

"The best present a mother could get is a few weddings and..."

The roars of "Mother!" deafened the room once more.

. . .

MAX WATCHED Greg rip the colorful wrapping paper off yet another present with enthusiasm. Greg's attention span was short; as soon as he started opening a new gift, he forgot what he had previously opened. But he was going home with a nice take.

Max remembered when he was a boy, wishing for certain gifts. His parents usually got him exactly what he had wanted—within reason, of course. Now he knew where all those letters to Santa went—in his father's pocket when Ron went Christmas shopping. His parents had always found a way to never disappoint their sons, even though they had never been rich.

Love had always been more important in the Bryson home than money. It still was.

His father lounged in his favorite recliner, trying to keep both eyes open but occasionally losing the fight. His mother was hovering over Amanda and Greg, her eyes lit with joy as she *oohed* and *aahed* over the boy's endless gifts, exciting Greg all the more. Max could tell his mother enjoyed having a child once again in the house, even though the "child" was in his early twenties.

When he had told his mother that he had invited both Amanda and Greg over for the holiday, Mary Ann had been ecstatic. She had run out immediately to purchase more presents. His mother made no bones about how nice it would be to have another female in the house. She mentioned time and time again how she was sick of being the lone women surrounded by a bunch of hardheaded males.

Max chuckled at the thought. He was suddenly the focus of everyone's attention.

"Something funny, brother?" Matt asked. Matt had become way too serious since going overseas. Max hoped he would snap out of it soon. His younger brother had been moody and quiet since his return home.

"No, nothing." Max was glad something had finally drawn

both his brothers' intense gazes from the attractive woman chatting with his mother.

But it didn't last long. As Amanda stood to gather the mountain of trash Greg had made from his gift-wrap massacre, all male eyes—including his pop's—returned to appreciating the tight ass in the short skirt. And when she bent over—

Max coughed sharply, getting his brothers' attention once more, and scowled purposely at them. He never should have told her to wear that skirt. His mistake.

His mother frowned at the loud noise. "Are you okay, Max? Are you getting sick?" She rushed over to place the back of her hand against his forehead.

Was he okay? Well, if she really wanted to know...

"I'm fine."

"You feel awfully warm."

"I don't think Max is getting sick, Mom," Marc chipped in, smirking. "There is another reason he's a bit heated."

"Oh? What reason?"

"Mother, the fire in here is just a little warm," Max appeased her.

Amanda straightened from throwing the wrapping paper into the fireplace. "Sorry, I thought you said to throw the paper in the fire."

Ron slammed his recliner into an upright position, an imposing sound that made all the brothers' spines straighten out of habit. "You're fine, girl. You just keeping doing what you're doing and ignore these...*boys*."

Max jumped up before Amanda had the opportunity to bend down again. His strangled "I'll do it" came out a little too loudly. He urged her back to the couch. "Have a seat and relax. You're our guest."

Ignoring the male laughter in the room, he finished gathering the crumpled paper, tossing it into the blaze. He was briefly mesmerized by the fire's colors as the paper burned.

"This is the life," Mary Ann cooed as she settled on the couch next to Amanda. She patted her on the knee. "What a nice holiday. My boys here all together and blessedly healthy. And now one of them actually brought home a girl."

Max groaned.

Matt grimaced. "Mom, we're not fifteen."

"I know. That's what I'm saying. It's about time you boys settle down and start thinking about having some chil—"

"Mare, I think I smell something burning," Ron interrupted quickly.

Mary Ann popped up and rushed with a worried look into the kitchen.

All three brothers simultaneously let out a relieved sigh. Amanda laughed at the obvious discomfort the men had of that subject.

Ron smiled. "You know, boys, sometimes I feel your pain. Anyway, come over here, girl." He patted the recliner's arm.

Amanda obediently rose from the couch, and when she neared, Ron wrapped an arm around her waist, giving her a slight squeeze. With his other hand he dug in between the cushion of the recliner's seat. He pulled out a long black velvet box.

"What do you think of this? Do you think she'll like it?" He opened the box to reveal a simple but elegant gold necklace with three gems dangling from it in different colors.

"It's beautiful," Amanda whispered.

"Each gem represents the birth month of these pigheaded boys."

"Well, then she will love it."

Max neared and leaned over Amanda's shoulder to peer into the box. "Very nice, Pop. When are you going to give it to her?"

"Later, when all the ruckus has died down." Ron cleared his throat roughly. "When we're alone."

"Well, I think that's very romantic of you," Amanda answered.

A blush crept over his father's already ruddy cheeks. Max was stunned. That had to be the first time he'd ever seen his father blush. He met Amanda's eyes over his father's head.

"I've got something for you." He grabbed her wrist and drew her out of Ron's hold, guiding her back to the comfortably worn couch.

"Max, I didn't get you anything."

"Doesn't matter. I didn't expect anything."

"But..."

"Do you want some privacy, Max?" Matt cut in.

He frowned at his meddling brothers. He wanted to wipe the ridiculous smirk from Marc's face. "Look, it's no big deal." He went over to the tree to pull a rectangular gift from under the fragrant branches. Max handed her the brightly wrapped present.

Greg squealed with delight upon seeing another unopened present and rushed over to sit beside his sister. "Lemme open..."

"Greg," Max said patiently. "This one is for your sister. Why don't you let her open it?"

Greg answered by sticking out his lower lip.

Marc intervened. "Greg, come over by the fire and show me the new comic books you got."

Greg grinned and rushed over to Marc, quickly forgetting his sister.

Max would have to remember to thank his brother later—even though it was the least Marc could do for being such a smart-ass. Max sank onto the couch next to Amanda. "Open it."

Amanda tentatively pulled back the paper to reveal a thick

hardcover book. It was a reference book on dealing with intellectually delayed adults.

She looked up and met Max's eyes. He cursed himself. He was stupid for getting her that gift. He should have gotten her something nicer. More personal. More...

"Real romantic, Max. Way to go," Matt chimed in acerbically.

"No, it's nice. Thank you." Amanda leaned over, bracing a hand on his thigh, and kissed him on the cheek. Her hand lingered just a second longer than was necessary.

Max felt the tightening in his groin and heat where her hand had been. He wanted more than a peck on the cheek or a brush of her hand on his thigh. If his family hadn't been present, he would have crushed her in an embrace to show her what he really wanted to give her. *Damn.* That wasn't a real "holiday" spirited notion.

Mary Ann's voice broke into his lewd thoughts. "Dinner's ready!"

Marc led Greg away, and Matt came over, offering his arm to escort Amanda into the dining room. Max continued to sit; he was unable to move until he could gain control of his mind and his body.

Amanda made him horny as hell.

Ron came over and slapped him on the back. "That's all right, son. You've got all the time in the world to impress that girl. Today just wasn't the time."

His father laughed as he strode away.

IT WAS LATE. Her stomach was painfully full. Greg was dozing off by the fire in his new NASCAR sweatshirt and baseball cap.

Amanda wondered if she would ever be able to get him out of those clothes again.

The men had carried the ridiculous number of gifts that Greg had received to the car, then suspiciously all disappeared.

Max stomped the newly fallen snow off his feet as he came back inside. She met him at the front door.

"I brushed off the car and started it so it would warm up."

"Thanks," she murmured as he helped her into her faux-fur jacket.

"I can follow you home."

"No, that's okay. I don't want to inconvenience you."

"It's not a problem. I'm going home anyway."

"Oh, you don't live here?"

Max chuckled and tilted her face up to his. "I haven't lived with my parents since I was eighteen. I have a house closer to town." He brushed a thumb over her bottom lip. "I'm glad you came."

"I am too."

He pointed to something over her head. She raised her eyes to the infamous mistletoe hanging above her.

She raised her eyebrows. He was going to kiss her? Here? In his parents' house?

Her eyelids dropped as his head lowered.

Oh yes. He was going to kiss her. No doubt about it.

Her heart pounded.

She shouldn't let him; her mind was saying it wasn't a good idea. Her body was saying otherwise.

His warm breath caressed her lips and mingled with hers. She waited. And waited. Her eyelids fluttered back open; the intensity of his ice-blue eyes bored into her. She tried to speak, but he swiftly crushed her lips with his. Angling his head, he ground his tongue with hers. She reached up to grip his shirt.

Oh. Yes.

He drove his fingers into her long auburn waves to pull her even closer. Then as quickly as it began, he pulled away, laying his forehead against hers, both of them panting softly.

That was even better than she'd dreamed.

Amanda unwound her fingers from the shirt fabric, brushing her hand down his broad chest, to his narrow waist and lower... Max grabbed her wrist tightly.

"I'm having a hard time controlling myself as it is."

She nodded slightly, touched her lips with shaky fingers, then turned away. She left him there and went to wake Greg, bundling him up in his heavy winter coat. Max continued to stand stiffly by the front door, silently watching her as they left. Legs trembling, she stepped out into the snow.

She gripped Greg's hand to help guide him over the slippery walkway to the car. The moonlight's reflection off the snow lit their way.

A fierce shiver ran up her spine.

Amanda wanted to think it was from the cold. But she knew better.

Chapter Six

As AMANDA DROVE down the lane, she realized she should have taken Max up on his offer of following her home. It had snowed a little more than she thought. Up until now she had driven in some dustings but not real snow.

When she got out to the main road, she panicked even further. The roads were not plowed. Or even salted.

She hoped the Buick could make it home. There was no way that she was going to turn around like a wuss and go back to the Bryson house. She would just take her time.

She glanced quickly at Greg before turning her gaze back to the road to concentrate. At least he had fallen back to sleep and wouldn't be harassing her about her driving.

The ride to the farm earlier in the day had only taken about twenty-five minutes. And here she was at least forty-five minutes later and still wasn't even close to being home.

Every time the rear end of the car slid she bit back a squeal. She wanted to avoid waking Greg.

Out of nowhere, headlights came up quickly behind her. Close enough to the point of tailgating. The lights were high, like from a truck, and their glare into the rearview mirror hurt her eyes. She wanted to wave the person around her, but she was afraid to take a hand off the wheel.

Then the honking began, making her jump. There was no traffic coming the other way; why didn't they go around?

The truck pulled around her and up next to her. She took a fleeting glance over.

Max.

She didn't know if she should be relieved or annoyed. He shouldn't have scared her like that.

He rolled down his passenger window, and she could barely hear him yelling at her to stop or pull over.

She did. She slammed on the brakes, and the Buick slid ten feet before coming to a stop crookedly in the middle of the road.

Max parked behind her and walked up to the car.

He stood there for a moment, and then when she didn't move, he tapped on the window with his knuckle.

"Roll down your window."

Amanda released the painful grip on the steering wheel to push the power window button.

He leaned into the window. "What are you doing?"

She gave him a look. "It's not obvious? I'm going home."

"You were driving five miles an hour."

"Oh."

"Amanda, there is only an inch of snow out here."

"Really?"

She heard his chuckle. She didn't think it was funny. Only an inch? It had seemed like a foot. *Shit.*

"I guess you've never driven in snow before."

"Not until coming up here."

"Hell, winter hasn't even started yet."

Great.

"I'll tell you what. I'll park my truck and drive the Buick

home for you." He nodded toward Greg. "I don't want to wake him up just to transfer him into my truck."

He did just that. Without even waiting for an answer from her, he went back to his vehicle, parked it off the roadway in a field, came back, and made her sit in the back since Greg was asleep in the passenger seat.

He drove the car back to her house without a word, but she could see the grin on his face and the looks that he kept giving her in the rearview mirror. He must think it was funny that she couldn't drive in the snow. She was just a helpless female.

With a straight face, she gave him the finger and slid over to the corner of the backseat so she was out of his view. A low chuckle came from the driver's seat.

She looked out the window and realized that they were already pulling into her driveway. He pushed the garage door opener and slipped the car inside before turning off the ignition and shutting the garage door again.

He got out and went around to the passenger side and quietly woke up Greg. Max helped Greg out of the car. Amanda remained in the backseat watching this man take her brother into the house. He clearly had a soft spot for Greg. She had to admit that there was more to him than met her eye. All business on the outside, but on the inside? He was someone who cared enough to include Greg and her for Christmas with his family, and afterward go out of his way to make sure they got home safely. He didn't have to do either. But he did.

However, she didn't want to rely on anyone other than herself. She needed to be more independent. How was she going to achieve that if he kept stepping in to save her ass?

She had been dependent for most of her life; now she needed to be the complete opposite.

But, honestly, as much as it irked her that he had to drive them home, she was relieved he had. Not that she was going to tell him that. She didn't want him to think he could step in whenever he damn well pleased.

Not even five minutes later, Max came back into the garage and stared at her through the car window. "Are you going to sit in there all night?"

She gave him a slight shoulder shrug.

He opened the back door and slid in next to her.

"Amanda—"

"You think I'm helpless, don't you?"

He gave her a surprised look. "Why would you think that?"

"I could have driven home myself."

"Okay," he said cautiously. "And your point is?"

"My point is that I *should* have gotten us home. I shouldn't have needed your help. I need to learn to do things on my own. Like driving in a little bit of snow."

"Really? Because at the rate you were going, you would still be out there miles away." He slid his fingers along her jawline, pushing a tendril of hair behind her ear. "Don't be so hard on yourself. Yes, you should definitely be able to drive in snow, but, hell, tonight wasn't a good night for practice. Especially with Greg in the car. I could help you learn, if you want."

Amanda flattened her lips and looked out of the opposite window, away from him. He was throwing himself in the mix again.

Though she was flattered he wanted to help, but...she wanted to stand on her own two feet, not have a man propping her up. Max grabbed her chin and turned her toward him. "Amanda. I only wanted to help. It's my job." *I'm here to protect and serve.*

She pulled her chin out of his fingers and met his eyes. "I'm not your job," she whispered.

He didn't say anything for a moment, just looked at her. She couldn't read him. She wanted to know what he was thinking.

He reached out a hand, then captured her wrist quickly.

Pulling it to his mouth, he brushed his lips lightly against her pulse.

"I know," he said finally.

She closed her eyes against the heat she saw in his.

"Amanda...look at me."

She opened her eyes and murmured, "You have no way to get home."

"I don't care." He brushed his lips against her fingers.

"I... I forgot to thank you for including us today—" He stopped her words with a thumb against her lips. His thumb continued across her lower lip, along her jawline, and then his fingers found their way into her hair. "And..." She sighed. "And for driving us home."

"Was my pleasure."

He made a fist, grasping and pulling, tugging her head back, exposing her neck. He leaned in, nuzzling her throat. His warm tongue stroked her skin.

She gasped as wetness pooled between her legs. Her breasts ached for his touch. She needed him deep inside her.

He nibbled along the neck of her sweater, around the hollows of her collarbone.

He sat up suddenly, pulling her roughly into his lap. Her miniskirt bunched at her hips as she straddled him in the backseat of the boring Buick.

Only it wasn't so boring at the moment.

The hard line of his cock was distinct through his jeans. She could feel it nestled along her sensitive heat, her thin stockings no protection at all.

Max ran his hands along her back to slide under her soft sweater. The roughness of his fingers against her heated skin made her grind a little against him.

"Fuck," he groaned, thrusting up just a little himself.

He reached higher along her back to release her bra, then slid his hands around to push the front of her sweater and her bra up, exposing her breasts to him.

"Perfect," he whispered.

She wanted his mouth on her. Wanted him to suck her. To take each nipple in his mouth and tug on them hard. Wanted him to nip her and nuzzle...

Amanda grabbed his face and ripped his gaze from her breasts. His eyes were hooded and unreadable. With a groan, she plundered his mouth. Their lips crushed together, their tongues fought, and she held his face tightly, not letting him go, not letting him escape.

He found both of her nipples with his fingers and tweaked them. Pulling, pinching, twisting, making her squirm in his lap.

His cock hard, his jeans were rough and irritating through her stockings and panties, but she didn't care. It felt good. She thrust against him harder. She thought she heard a tear. But, again, she didn't care.

All she wanted at this moment was to get closer. Eat him up. Take control of his mouth as their lips meshed. She pulled back only to say, "Harder."

He did what she asked. He pinched her nipples harder, pulled harder, twisted harder.

She had to give his mouth up. She had to let him go to gasp against his neck. She shuddered against him, tilting her hips, feeling his hard cock so close but not close enough.

Still hiding her face against his shoulder, she grasped the snap to his jeans and pulled. It gave away, but the zipper was tougher. The pressure of his cock against it made it difficult to manipulate.

Before she could finish, he had his large hands on her hips and had her flipped under him on the backseat. Max settled between her legs and captured her wrists, holding her still.

"Do you know what you're asking for?"

Of course! she wanted to scream. But instead, she choked out a *yes*.

He tightened his hold on her wrists and stretched her arms over her head. "Do you like it rough?"

Amanda's heart skipped a beat. "Oh yes."

Max's smile grew.

His cell phone, which he had thrown in the console earlier, blared an obnoxious country tune.

Max frowned, but didn't move.

Amanda pulled on her wrists and thrust against him to remind him what they'd been doing. What she wanted him to continue with.

The tune stopped, and the phone beeped to indicate a voice-mail message.

Max's icy blue eyes pinned her. He transferred both of her wrists to one hand and worked the other one between them until he found the hole in her stocking, which was in a *very* convenient place. Right at her crotch.

He dug his fingertips into the hole and pulled, ripping the hole bigger, giving him more access to what was beneath. He maneuvered his fingers into her stockings enough to yank her panties to the side and then plunged two fingers deep within her. His fingers met no resistance. She was slick and hot.

"You're so fucking wet," he said between gritted teeth. "So fucking wet. Jesus."

Amanda gasped with the pleasure of his fingers ramming in and out of her. It wasn't enough. "Do you think you're man enough for me?"

He suddenly stopped. A slight hesitation. She had caught him off guard.

"Baby, I'm all you'll ever need."

"Then show me."

Max's cell phone blared that stupid tune again, making him

yell out a curse. He jerked away from her and snatched up his phone. "What, Marc?"

Amanda took a deep breath. Trying to catch her wits. What were they doing? They were in the backseat of the car, which was parked in the garage. With Greg just upstairs.

"Yes, I'm fine... No, I left my truck there... I did not wreck it... Amanda needed help getting home."

Amanda stiffened and pulled her knees up, making Max unbalanced. He had to move off her completely to finish his conversation.

"Uh. I guess... Okay. How soon? You are?" Amanda watched Max tense and scrub at his short hair in agitation with his hand. "Sure." Max hit the End button with more pressure than was needed and turned his head to look at Amanda. "Marc is parked out in your driveway."

"What?" She sat up quickly, straightening her miniskirt and what was left of her stockings.

"He said if I'm not out there in five minutes, he's coming in." He frowned. "I'm going to kill him."

Amanda rehooked her bra, wiggled her breasts back into the cups, and tugged her sweater down. "Why is he here?"

"He saw my truck abandoned in the field and got worried. He saw two sets of tracks nearby in the snow, so he figured your car was the second vehicle."

"Oh. Well, shit."

"Shit is right. He's going to give me a ride back to my truck."

"Oh."

"*Jesus Christ.* Is that all you can say?" He reached down in his jeans and adjusted himself before zipping them closed and fastening the snap. His movements were jerky, and his jaw was clenched. She wondered who he was angry at. Her? Marc? Himself?

"What do you want me to say?"

"That you're disappointed?"

"I..." *Am. I want to fuck your brains out. There...are you happy?* "Well, maybe it's better this way."

He looked at her in disbelief. "Better?"

"Look at us. We are in the backseat of a car. We don't even really like each other."

"We don't?"

"Well, no. I think you're way too bossy, and you think I'm irresponsible and immature." *Excuses, excuses.* But she refused to let on how disappointed she was.

"Amanda—"

Max's phone rang again, and he flipped, cursing his brother up one side and down the other. He pushed the door open and climbed out of the back of the car. He grabbed his coat, which he had removed sometime earlier, and shoved his arms into the sleeves.

"I'll talk to you later. I have to go commit murder."

"Merry Christmas," she called out. She was answered by the slam of the side door to the garage.

Her dreams were going to be torture tonight.

Chapter Seven

HER CART WAS near to overflowing. Jars of peanut butter, pounds and pounds of butter, bags of flour, eggs, milk... Amanda looked down at her list. She still needed to hit the meat department. She had dug out a Crock-Pot from the back of a cabinet after finding an easy recipe to try in the slow cooker. It had only listed a handful of ingredients and not much preparation. She could handle that. But shopping, on the other hand...

Her grocery list was three pages long—both sides. She had already spent forty-five minutes in the retail giant. She couldn't imagine what her bill would be when she checked out.

And to top everything off, she had picked a cart with a defective wheel. So every few feet it would stick and squeal like a stuck pig when she continued to push. She gritted her teeth.

The wheel jammed again as she tried to take a corner into the next aisle. She shoved harder, and the wheel freed abruptly, the cart escaping her grip.

She winced as it had a head-on collision with another shopper's cart. As the other shopper gave her an evil look, she apologized profusely. "I'm so sorry. The damn—dang wheel stuck."

The harried young mother tightened her hold on the toddler by her side. She looked like she was about to give Amanda a piece of her mind.

"I guess I'm going to have to write up a crash report. Do I need to call rescue?" Max rolled his cart up next to the "crash" scene. To Amanda, it looked as if rescue had already arrived.

"It's okay, Mrs. Leonard. I'll take over from here. You're free to go." He leaned down to the toddler, chucking him under the chin. "And you too, Jessie."

Mrs. Leonard picked up her child and put him in the cart. As she rolled away, the woman grumbled, "You should write her a ticket for reckless driving, Max."

Max gave Mrs. Leonard an easy smile. "I'll do that." He then shifted his attention to Amanda, his smile slipping a bit.

"What are you doing here?" Amanda's cheeks burned. What a stupid question.

"Shopping?" He scanned the contents of her cart. "What are *you* doing? Opening a restaurant?"

"No. I have some recipes I'm working on, and I needed some ingredients. I bought a bunch of cookbooks at a church sale."

He snagged a jar of the peanut butter. "Apparently. Ten jars of peanut butter? You must be making some more of your great peanut butter cookies. You can drop them off at the station anytime. We all loved them."

"Uh, sure, I'll do that." The heat that had left her cheeks a second earlier returned in full force. She needed to change the subject. She eyed his cart. Vegetable juice, "healthy" frozen meals, a variety of fruits, and a gallon of skim milk barely filled the bottom. Not a doughnut to be found in this cop's diet. "Watching your weight?"

"I always watch my girlie figure," Max joked.

His figure looked good to Amanda. Extremely fine. His hard lines and masculine angles looked downright—

"Amanda?"

"Hmm?" She drew her attention from the snug fit of his jeans back up to his face. Well, almost. Her gaze stuck on the bulge of his biceps through his long-sleeved cotton shirt. Then she finally met his gaze.

"I have to go. I'm working second shift." He didn't move. "If you need someone to taste test those recipes, I'm available."

"I'll let you know."

"You have my cell."

"Yep."

"I keep it on all the time."

"No kidding."

"I have to because of my job..." His voice died away. Max shifted closer, their gazes locking.

Amanda said softly, "I'm sure." Was he going to kiss her? Here? In the cereal aisle at Walmart?

"Okay, I have to go."

"Me too." He was going to kiss her. Her lips parted in anticipation.

"I'll see you later," he said in a husky whisper.

"Okay." Her heart hammered.

Instead he ran his thumb over her lips. "Keep out of trouble." He pulled reluctantly away.

"Right." The break of contact left her feeling cold. *Damn.* "Max?"

He stilled. "Yeah?"

She gave him a tentative smile. "Stay safe."

He answered with one of his own. "I will."

Then he was gone, leaving Amanda standing alone by the shredded wheat, wondering where this was going to go. And how soon.

AMANDA PULLED the plain Buick into the garage and popped the trunk release. She needed to get the groceries unloaded and put away before Greg got home. Even though her brother tried to be helpful after she went grocery shopping, it never failed that eggs got smashed, a grocery bag broke, or a dozen apples scattered out of the garage and down the driveway. He meant well, but...

As she came around the back of the car, she noticed Max's truck pulling in.

What the hell?

He jumped out of his Chevy and yelled, "Hey, you forgot something!"

Her brows knit together as she patted her pockets. Did she forget her credit card at the store?

He rushed up to her, making her step back in surprise. "What did I forget?"

"This," he stated as he pulled her into his arms and captured her lips with his.

Oh yes. Damn her forgetfulness.

His mouth slanted over hers, their tongues tangling and twisting. He pulled her hips against him, and she could feel his hardness through his jeans press against her lower belly.

He swept his fingers through her hair, pulling her head back even more, exposing her neck. He licked her bottom lip, then trailed his tongue down her neck, over the rapid pulse along her throat. He finished with a kiss at the curve of her throat.

"You don't know how badly I want to finish what we started in the back of that damn Buick."

A shiver went down Amanda's spine. *Oh, me too.*

The crack of a screen door slamming had them both looking at each other before looking over at Mrs. Busybody's house.

"Shit," Max whispered.

"I thought you had to go to work."

"I do." He glanced at his watch. "I'll make it on time. I

wanted to help you unload all the groceries you bought. And... and I wanted to kiss you. I hesitated in the store, and I regretted it."

"What about your groceries?" Through his windshield, she could see the bags on the passenger side of his truck cab.

"I'll throw them in the fridge at the station."

Max could grab more bags at a time than Amanda ever could, and within minutes they had unloaded everything onto the kitchen counters.

As she turned to thank him, his arms came around her from behind, pulling her against him.

"I don't want to go to work. I want to stay here and bury myself deep inside you."

Her pussy throbbed at the vision his words put into her head. Yes, she wanted that too.

He ran his palm over her jeans until he cradled her pussy in his hand. She gasped when his fingers played with her nipples through her sweater. They were hard and tight, and she wanted his mouth on them. She wanted him to suckle and squeeze them. He nibbled along her neck down to her exposed collarbone. The wide-necked sweater gave him enough access to run his tongue along her delicate skin before ending it with a kiss.

With a groan, he pulled away. "I gotta go before I'm late and my ass is in a sling with Dunn, since I'm relieving him."

Amanda straightened her sweater and cursed the wetness between her legs. She might have to go change her panties when he left.

"I take dinner break around seven. I can stop by. Would you be interested in making a hungry, hardworking man some supper?"

Amanda had a flash of panic. Oh, he did not want her cooking for him. At least not yet. Even though she was trying to teach herself to cook, she had a long way to go yet.

"I... I know I just bought all these groceries, but I was just planning on picking up pizza for Greg and me. I was going to keep it simple tonight." Good save, she thought.

"Then how about I pick up pizza and I'll be here around seven. As long as I don't get a last minute emergency call, that is. I'll text you if I'm running late."

Before she could even agree to the dinner date, he was rushing out of the house. A few seconds later, she heard his truck tires pealing down the road.

Amanda touched her lips and smiled.

Greg ran to the door when the headlights of the cruiser lit up the front of the house.

"Max here! Max here!"

Chaos echoed his owner's excitement, circling and barking at the front door.

"Chaos!" Amanda yelled from the kitchen. "Greg, go out and help Max with the pizza."

Amanda felt the draft of cold air as Greg rushed out the front door, leaving it wide open, Chaos hot on his heels.

He probably hadn't even bothered to put shoes on. Amanda sighed.

Within minutes, three males took over her kitchen. One barking. One bouncing, talking a mile a minute, and wringing his hands. And one...

Amanda stopped setting out the napkins and straightened. *Oh yeah.*

And one wearing that dark blue uniform of his, making him look sharp and put together like no man she'd ever seen before. Studying him, she could see why women liked men in uniform.

Both Greg and Max were carrying a pizza box, so she took

the one from Greg and put it on the table before it ended upside down on the floor. Max slid his on top of the other.

He reached for the mic at his shoulder and pushed the button. "Dispatch from Manning Grove eight."

The radio squawked loudly throughout the room. Greg's eyes lit up and widened, and he shifted foot to foot. "Manning Grove eight, go ahead."

"Dispatch, I'll be ten-six for dinner. I'll be on portable."

"Ten-four, Manning Grove eight."

Max unhooked the mic from his shoulder and the radio from his hip, placing both on the counter nearby.

"Oh, can... can... can I's speak on that?"

Before Max could answer, Amanda stepped in. "No, Bud, that's not a toy. Only Max gets to use the radio."

Greg rolled his eyes, disappointed. "Awwwww."

"Go wash your hands." She shooed him to the sink. "Holy crap, Chaos, settle down."

The dog finally sat, his tail thumping against the linoleum floor. She swore the dog just smiled at her knowingly. She shook her head and looked back at Max.

Max leaned in close to kiss her on the cheek. She wanted a more thorough kiss, but she could understand him keeping it on the more conservative side since they had an audience. Who was like a sponge.

"Is that a gun on your hip or are you just happy to see me?" she asked him in a low voice.

He leaned in close again and whispered in her ear, "Both."

"Gun! Can... can I's hold it? Max? Max! Can I?"

"*No!*" They both answered at the same time. Apparently she hadn't kept her voice low enough. She took a mental note.

Greg pouted. "Why not?"

Max went over to the sink to wash his hands while lecturing Greg. "Guns are dangerous, Greg. You have to have a lot of training before you can hold one. You don't want to hurt anyone by accident, do you?"

"No," Greg answered with an exaggerated shake to his head. "But..."

Amanda needed to change the subject before Greg played twenty questions on why he couldn't handle Max's gun. "So, Manning Grove eight, what kind of pizza did you get?"

"I wasn't sure what you liked, so I did one half mushrooms, half pepperoni, and the other just plain cheese."

"That's a lot of pizza for only three people."

"Well, Greg and I are still growing boys."

Greg plopped down in a chair at the table. "Yeah, 'Manda, Max an' I's are growin' boys."

Max wiggled his eyebrows at Amanda. Yeah, she knew exactly where he was still growing. And it wasn't his height.

Within minutes, Max had scarfed down three slices and Greg was trying to keep up, though while Max tended to use a napkin, Greg had sauce ringing his mouth as he shoved in a piece of crust.

Greg blasted out a belch so loud Chaos started barking.

"Manners." Amanda scolded him.

But Max laughed in turn, making Greg laugh around his apology. "'Scuze me."

She gave Max the side eye. "Don't encourage him."

Max just shrugged. He asked Greg, "Do you feel better?"

Greg nodded his head as he chewed on another piece of crust.

Max winked at Amanda. "Good."

"How long is your dinner break?"

"As long as the radio is quiet."

Which, of course, jinxed him. The radio suddenly chirped, and Max already was out of his seat. "Dispatch to Manning Grove eight."

Max grabbed the portable. "Manning Grove eight. Go."

"Two vehicle crash at Williams Road and Hollow Hill Lane. Unknown injuries. Fire and EMS en route."

Amanda watched as his whole demeanor changed suddenly from the relaxed pizza-eating guy seconds ago to shoulder-squared, protect-and-serve guy now. She even thought his chest puffed out a little bit more.

"Ten-four, dispatch. I'll be en route."

"Can I's go with Max?"

Amanda brushed his hair out of his eyes as they watched Max shrug on his heavy patrol jacket. "No, Bud. Sometimes we need to handle things on our own."

Max gave her an apologetic smile before heading out the door.

Well, shit.

While Amanda started to clean up the table, her cell phone beeped. She checked her texts.

Meet me in your driveway at 11:15.

THE MAN WAS prompt if nothing else.

Amanda slid into the passenger side of Max's Chevy pickup. Only the glow of his dashboard illuminated the interior once she quietly shut the door. Last thing she wanted was to wake up Greg. Or the neighbors. Like Mrs. Busybody.

He was back in his civilian clothes, soft worn jeans, and a short-sleeved T-shirt, exposing the Marine tattoo on his arm. Amanda wanted to lean over and lick it. And that would just be the starting point.

"You know it's like negative twenty degrees out there."

Max's chuckle was low, causing a shiver to run down her

83

spine and her pussy to quiver. "It's thirty-eight degrees. My jacket's behind the seat, and I have the heat on."

She tilted her head and studied his strong jawline and lips that were curved up in a smile.

"I may have to turn the heat off if you don't stop looking at me like that."

She placed a palm on his chest over the thin cotton. "You do feel a bit warm."

He wrapped his fingers with hers, bringing her wrist to his mouth. He pressed his lips against her skin and stroked his tongue over her pulse point.

"I want to get to know you better, Amanda..."

The way he hesitated after her name made her think, *uh-oh.* This wasn't going to be as simple as it could be.

"But?"

She pulled her hand back when he sighed, letting it fall to her lap.

"But my parents really like you."

Amanda shook herself mentally. What? "And that's a problem, how?"

"Listen. I've been a bachelor my whole life."

Oh, here we go.

"I mean, I date—have dated. But between my stint in the Marines right after high school, going through the police academy, then concentrating on my career, I just never had the desire to get serious with anyone."

"Who said anything about being serious?" Amanda's stomach churned. Where the hell was this going?

"No one... yet." Max cleared his throat and stared at the hands he now had gripping the steering wheel. "Here's the deal..."

She stared at his profile, wishing he would get to the point. This was getting painful. "Okay, so you just want to fuck me and not have anything serious. No problem. I'm completely fine with that. You come over, fuck me until I come, then you go home."

His head swiveled toward her, wearing a frown. "No—"

"Yes. I get it. You just want an occasional booty call."

"No. Wait. Hear me out."

"What, Max? What do you want? What are you trying to say?"

"You heard my parents...No, my mom on Christmas Day, so excited to see a female in her house. She has been bugging all of us to settle down, produce children. I mean it's a constant thing when we're there."

"Okay, I get it. I'm not the one you want to settle down and have children with."

"No. Well, yes... No! Fuck!" Max scrubbed a hand over his short, bristly hair. "No. I just don't want to give her the wrong idea. Like I said, I want to get to know you better, but I... I... just don't need the pressure from my mother."

"So, you're saying you're a pussy and can't stand up to your mother."

Max pinched the bridge of his nose and just shook his head.

"You're saying that if you're seeing someone, your mom suddenly hears wedding bells."

Max sighed, letting out a long shaky breath.

"You're saying that you're afraid to fuck someone casually because you're going to be pressured by your mom to start popping out brats if she finds out."

Amanda laughed, and Max's eyebrows shot to the top of his head.

"You know you can be a control freak, but it sounds like you get it honestly. You like to control others, but you're afraid of your mother controlling you." She was being a little harsh. She knew what a real controlling mother was like. She had one of her very own. Her mother was a controlling, manipulative woman, but she didn't see Mary Ann as that at all. "From the little that I saw, she only wants what's best for you. Just like a good mother should. You're very lucky to have her."

"I am lucky to have her. And my pop. But I think you're missing my point."

"No. I get it. You want to fuck me, but you want us to keep in on the DL. I got it totally."

"Just from my parents."

She knew what he was getting at, but he was not going to be getting any help from her to pull the foot out of his mouth.

"You really don't want my mom to start meddling and blowing things out of proportion. My mom doesn't know why anyone would want to take it slow or get to know someone better first. So that's a reason to keep it on the DL."

"You know, there was this cop who once told me that this was a small town, and everybody knows everyone's business," she teased.

He snorted and shook his head. "I'm such an ass."

She smiled. "I won't argue that fact. But you do have a very hot ass and I do want to fuck you and I don't want to marry you or start popping out your spawn. So now what?"

"So now we get naked and fuck?" he suggested. He gave her a sheepish grin, which totally melted her heart.

"Here? Is that even possible in the cab of a pickup?"

"Oh yeah. Anything is possible if you want it badly enough."

"So, Officer Bryson, are you saying you want me bad?"

"I want you so badly I can taste it."

Amanda chuckled. "Well, tasting is good." She looked around the cramped quarters of the truck. "But I still don't know how this would work."

Max tilted the steering wheel up, making a smidgeon more room. He twisted in the driver's seat to face her. He stroked his thumb over her lower lip gently.

Driving his fingers into her long hair, he pulled her close. He murmured against her lips, "I want to make you come. I want to hear you cry out. I want to hear you scream my name."

That sounded like a good plan to her.

He smothered her lips with his, and Amanda sighed, her breath blending with his, her tongue brushing against his. And as he deepened the kiss, her nipples hardened painfully under her sweater.

He pulled back, breaking their kiss. "You see that handle up there? Grab that and lift yourself up so I can slide over."

She pulled herself up and he slid under her, but before she could settle in his lap, he grabbed her yoga pants and pulled them down her legs. She was so glad she had changed into the comfier, easier-to-remove pants. Plus, she never wore panties under her yoga pants. He threw them onto the driver's seat along with her sneakers.

She released the grab handle and yanked her sweater over her head. Oh yeah, she had also removed her bra when she had changed. She had been thinking.

Before she could turn, he ran his hand over her hip and then down to find the V of her legs. Her thighs trembled as he explored her, his fingers separating her, pressing her clit, before dragging between her swollen lips to discover her wetness. She bit her lip and closed her eyes. She slammed her palms down on the dash to steady herself, and her head fell forward as he pressed his fingers inside her. She was so hot, so wet, that he whispered those words into her skin as he licked and kissed along her spine.

He twisted a nipple with one hand while his other fucked her over and over until her knees buckled and she fell back against him, crying out.

"Turn around." His voice was harsh. Commanding. And it made the heat at her core want to explode.

She twisted in his arms, in his lap, until she straddled him.

His eyelids were heavy, his breathing ragged, and his hard-on was unmistakable in his jeans.

He kissed her long and deep, finally releasing her so he could kiss down her neck, finding the hollow of her throat. He cupped her breast and lowered his head, sucking the nipple between his lips.

Her back arched; she wanted him to suck harder, pinch harder, pull and tease her nipple.

He did all that. And more. Nipping, caressing, licking her skin, biting her shoulder, stroking her clit with his thumb.

She needed him now. Inside her. Otherwise, she was going to break apart and go mad.

"I want you. Now." She groaned and lifted herself up again, trying to give him enough space to pull his jeans down. He managed to push them to just past his knees before sinking back in the seat and taking her with him. His thighs were big and muscular, so when her knees found enough purchase to straddle him, she spread wide, inviting, waiting.

He took a handful of her ass, pulling her tight against him. He fisted the base of his cock, and she shifted until the tip was at her entrance. And when she let her body go, she sank down on him, taking him inside her completely.

She tilted her hips just slightly, seating him even deeper. She had him all, from base to tip, inside her.

He dug his fingers into the flesh around her hips as she lifted and fell, riding his pulsing cock.

He watched her watching him. She wanted to smile at him, tell him how good this felt, how hard he was, how wet she was for him. But nothing came out but nonsense. Curses. Groans. Cries. He joined her, wordless sounds as she rode him hard.

Until she squeezed her inner walls tight around him. And he stilled, his nostrils flaring, his eyes closed, his jaw tight.

She squeezed his cock like a fist, releasing and tightening.

Release. Tighten.

She ground her hips down against him. Once. Twice. The pleasure built until it radiated from her core, curling her toes, making her eyes roll back in her head.

With one last cry, her body pulsated around him, her climax spiraling from her center.

He threw his head back against the seat. "Fuck!" And he released deep inside her.

She dropped her forehead onto his shoulder and let out a long, shaky breath.

SHE LAID with her head in his lap as he sat up in the driver's seat. Her legs were folded against the passenger-side door, and her muscles complained a little in that cramped position. The gear shifter was jammed into her ribs, but it was worth it because he was stroking her hair while she stared up at him. They hadn't said anything for a while, and she didn't want to break the easy silence. His fingers in her hair made her want to purr.

His other hand moved down her skewed sweater to draw circles around her bare belly button. At the end of every circle he would flick the gold hoop at the center.

"What's your dream, Mandy?"

Her thoughts were slow and relaxed, and that was the last question she expected from Mr. Type A personality. Her dream...

"I don't know. Though, if you would have asked me a few months ago when my life was totally different, I still wouldn't have had an answer. I had no direction. I just lived day by day. Hour by hour. Partying with my friends, bartending for some cash, hanging out at nightclubs or in South Beach. Wherever the action was." She sighed. "Now I just feel lost."

"You're not lost."

"I feel like my feet were ripped out from under me during a riptide."

"You'll find your footing again."

"Maybe when I get back home." To Miami. Back to familiar things. Familiar ways. "What's your dream?"

"I'm living it."

She shifted her head to get a better view of his face. "Really? Wearing a uniform, arresting people, rescuing cats from trees?"

"Having a career I can be proud of. One with job security. Working on my pension so I can afford to eventually retire. Owning a home. Helping people. Saving enough that if my parents need help later in life, I can do that."

Amanda faked a yawn. "Sounds exciting."

Max shook his head. He gazed down into her face, studying her. "You're young yet."

"I'm twenty-eight."

"Age is just a number. You are young; in a few years you'll get what I'm saying."

"I don't know. Doesn't sound like my kind of life."

He took a deep breath. "Right." He looked at his watch. "Shit. It's one a.m. I need to get some sleep."

Amanda yawned. For real this time. "Yeah, me too. I used to stay out all night, but now I couldn't do it if I tried. Greg gets me up so early. My ass is going to be dragging in the morning."

She sat up and straightened her clothes before sliding out of the passenger-side door.

"I'll see you around, Officer Bryson."

"Hey," he called to her.

"Yeah?"

"Stay out of trouble."

"Why? I now have an 'in' at the local police department." With a wink, she slammed the door shut and ran into the house.

Chapter Eight

"The best home cooking is passed down through generations."

"Well, there aren't any good cooks in my family tree," Amanda told Mary Ann as they stood in the Amanda's kitchen.

"Nonsense. I can't believe that your mother never taught you anything in the kitchen."

"If you met her, you wouldn't even wonder."

Mary Ann bit into one of the cookies still on the plate, which had been carelessly tossed on the counter after Amanda's return from the neighbor's. "Oh dear."

She ripped a paper towel off the roll, carefully spitting out the mouthful. She wadded it up and tossed it in the garbage.

Amanda grimaced. She thought she had improved at least a little bit, especially since she stopped burning them after the first few dozen. Hence the desperate phone call to Max's mom. But Mary Ann's expression just proved it; Amanda was hopeless in the kitchen.

"Oh, sweetie, it's not that bad. Okay, well, it's not that good either. But it was a good try. You just need a little... uh, maybe a lot... of guidance. I'm so glad you called me. Now we get to spend some time together. I want to get to know you so much better. Especially since you're seeing my son."

"Well, we're not really—"

The older woman waved a hand at her. "Okay, we'd better get started. We have a *lot* of work to do."

They dug through all the cookbooks that Amanda had not only found in the house but also the stack of books she had bought at the church sale. The sale where Mary Ann had run into her and was kind enough to offer to help her learn to cook. *If* she needed it. And clearly she did.

The first lesson didn't even involve heat, fire, or anything burning. Mary Ann sat with Amanda to go through her extensive cookbook collection, pointing out easy recipes to try, explaining techniques that were involved, telling her more about some of the ingredients, and showing her the difference between cooking utensils.

The time flew, but there was so much to learn that Amanda's head started to ache. Mary Ann wanted to concentrate on baking first, but Amanda begged her to teach both cooking and baking at the same time so she could cook healthy meals for Greg. Mary Ann reluctantly relented and decided that each time they got together, whether here or on the farm, she would teach Amanda one dish and one baked good.

Amanda did know how to brew coffee, and she did so while they sat at the kitchen table mulling over future recipes.

Late in the afternoon, both were burned out. Amanda took a sip of the steaming-hot java. "Do you know your initials spell MA? Mary Ann. Ma."

Mary Ann chuckled, reminding Amanda of her son. "Of course I knew that."

"So, can I call you Ma for short? Would you mind?"

"Sweetie, I don't mind at all. I'd love it. You call me whatever you'd like." Mary Ann sighed and looked sightlessly over her mug. "I've always regretted not having a daughter. I just couldn't risk having another son. Three was enough. I told Ron that if he got me pregnant again, I'd castrate him myself. He was always such a randy man. Still is. And his sons are just like him. God help the women they choose. Hardheaded, harebrained—" She stopped abruptly as if suddenly remembering who she was with. "Oops, I should be pointing out his good points. I'm never going to get them married off if I tell the truth." Mary Ann laughed so hard she had to set her coffee down. "Well, I've got to get home and make my man some dinner. He gets pretty cranky if he doesn't get his supper on time." Mary Ann pushed away from the table and stood.

"I can't thank you enough for this."

"Not a problem. Why don't we just plan on meeting in a couple days? I'll give you some homework." She pushed two open cookbooks toward Amanda. "Have these two recipes ready for next time. We'll see how you do."

"Thanks, Ma."

After Mary Ann left, Amanda sat back. Her heart sang with delight. It felt really satisfying to spend time with Max's mother.

She had a feeling Max wasn't going to like the idea.

But then, who was going to tell him?

THE JINGLING of the bells followed her into the salon. Teddy looked up from the head he was washing and gave her a big smile.

"Hey, girlfriend."

"Hey, yourself."

He stuck out his lower lip in a mock pout. "Why so gloomy?"

"Bored to tears. Did I tell you that Mrs. Bryson is teaching me how to cook?"

Teddy raised a brow. "I think you left that one out."

"Yeah, and I'm not doing too badly, either, but... you can only spend so much time in the kitchen."

"So why not get a job?"

"Dealing with Greg *is* a job."

"No, seriously. Something part-time, something to keep you busy while he's at day care. I'd hire you, but I don't have enough clients. Now if the barbershop down the street ever closed, I'd probably be swamped and would need your help washing heads."

Amanda wrinkled her nose. "Yuck. I'm not washing people's hair." She looked at the older woman whose head he was scrubbing in the sink. "No offense."

The woman huffed her displeasure.

"Not good enough for you?" Teddy asked.

Amanda ignored that. "I just need to have some fun."

"That Bryson buck not keeping you busy enough?"

Amanda flushed as Teddy's client lifted her head a little, just enough to make sure she didn't miss any of the latest gossip.

Amanda turned away to look at herself in a nearby mirror. "I don't know what you're talking about. Someone must have given you some bad information."

"Yeah. Whatever." He rinsed out the lady's blue hair. "Did you enjoy Egypt?"

"Egypt? I didn't go to Egypt."

"Oh, I thought you took a trip down denial."

Amanda turned away again to hide her laughter but realized that her image was reflected all over the shop. She stuck out her tongue at him, making him laugh.

"Go sit in that chair over there. I'll be done with Mrs. Anderson's hair in a flash. Then we can have a deep conversation. I don't have another appointment for forty-five minutes."

A deep conversation. All he would be doing is digging at her until she broke down and did a Catholic-like confession. "Oh Father, I have sinned..."

And he'd be lapping up every word of her "sins" like a kitten at a platter of cream. Not one drop would be wasted; he'd be licking his whiskers clean.

Amanda bit her lip at the imagery and wandered over to the waiting area.

No matter what, she was glad Teddy was here in Manning Grove. He kept her grounded, if that was possible. And neatly groomed. He always experimented on her with hair and makeup, giving her manicures and pedicures whenever he needed a guinea pig.

She sank into one of the upholstered chairs that looked like they dated back to the 1950s. Yesterday's newspaper had been thrown on a pile of hairstyle magazines, which teetered precariously on a glass-and-chrome table. She snagged the paper and began to thumb through it. The want ads were pitiful.

A waitress needed for the diner. No.

A volunteer needed for the library. No.

A "lunch lady" needed for the elementary school. No way!

Amanda sighed. She didn't really need to work. She also didn't want to take away a job opportunity from someone else, since jobs were hard to come by around here. And learning to cook was filling up some of her time, but still...

She scanned the rest of the meager paper, and an ad caught her eye.

Crazy Pete's Bar.

Karaoke from 8-11 Wednesday nights. Ladies Night Mondays. Happy Hour—drinks half-price on Tuesdays. Wings and a bucket of beer special all day on Friday, New Year's Eve.

New Year's Eve. That was today.

Boy, she could use a night out to get that "Bryson buck" off her mind.

As soon as Teddy was done with Mrs. Anderson, he escorted

the woman out the door, then came over and dropped himself in the chair next to Amanda with a sigh.

"That woman's impossible. I tell her that a blue rinse is *soooo* out-of-date. She doesn't care. People are so behind the times here. But if it weren't for the old ladies in this town, I wouldn't have enough business. If there were more young people, then I'd—"

"Where's this Crazy Pete's? What other bars are around here?"

Teddy gave her a worried look. "Crazy Pete's? It's the *only* bar in town and, believe me, that one is all that's needed. It's over on Third Street."

"Want to go celebrate the New Year in with me?"

Teddy gave her a skeptical look. "It isn't Pete who's crazy, it's you! You expect an openly gay man to go to Crazy Pete's? No, thank you."

"Is it that bad?"

"Girlfriend, when I drive by, I don't even make eye contact with anyone coming out of there."

"You're kidding, right?"

"Yes, but I'm still not going. I have a date with that cute Ryan Seacrest."

Max's previous multiple warnings of "stay out of trouble" bounced through her head.

"Well, I am. I need to check out the nightlife around here."

"Honey, there's more nightlife out in the woods."

She jumped up. "Let's do my hair and nails."

Teddy clapped his hands in excitement. "Now you're talking sense. A manicure coming right up. I'll do you, if you do me!"

They both fell over each other in a fit of giggles.

AFTER LEAVING THE SALON, Amanda picked Greg up early from the day care. She needed to talk to Donna anyway.

When she stepped through the facility's doors, it reminded her of the first time she met her brother. And how scared she had been; not that she was completely full of confidence now.

She spotted Donna behind the front desk; she looked up in surprise from shuffling some paperwork. Amanda went over.

"Amanda, it's so good to see you. How have you been dealing with Greg? I had expected to get numerous calls from you. Actually I had expected you to be calling me every hour on the hour." The woman laughed, giving Amanda a genuine smile.

Amanda returned the gesture. "I'm sure you did. But we're doing fine. I'm learning things as I go." And trying not to poison him with my cooking, she added silently.

"Boy, does Greg just love you. He talks about you all the time."

"He does?"

"Yes, of course."

"And does he say nice things?"

Donna laughed again. "Yes. I'm glad things are working out for him. I was afraid there for a while." She took a deep breath. "So, you're just here to pick up Greg? He's in the back room having a snack."

"Yes. But really, I had a favor to ask of you. I'm wondering if there is someone you could recommend to stay with Greg when I can't be home." She didn't want to say *babysitter* since Greg was hardly a baby and she wasn't sure if it was the right term to use.

"Like a sitter?"

Amanda sighed in relief. "Yes, exactly."

"Well, there's Joni. She's just a few years younger than you, and she works here part-time. So, she knows Greg and Greg knows her. I'd say she'd be perfect. She could probably use the extra money also."

"Great. Is she here?"

"No, not today due to the holiday. Let me give you her phone number." Donna grabbed a nearby Rolodex and flipped through it. "Here it is." She scribbled a number on a pad and ripped off the sheet to hand it to Amanda.

"Thank you. I'll call her right now." Amanda pulled her cell phone out of her bag.

"I'll get Greg ready to go while you're doing that."

Within a couple minutes Amanda had Joni set up to stay with Greg that night. She was going out. She was going to have a good time and no one—not even someone who wore a blue uniform and whose initials were M.B.—was going to stop her.

Chapter Nine

If drool wasn't running down the chin of every man in the bar, Max would be surprised.

He wiped his own.

Max lifted the beer bottle to his lips, the cool liquid slithering down his throat. Unfortunately, it did nothing to lower his body temperature.

"Damn!" His brother swore next to him as he knocked Max with his elbow. "Have you hit that yet?"

Marc was staring at exactly what he was staring at—Amanda Barber in a short, short—*very short*—skirt bent over a pool table attempting to make a nearly impossible shot. The solid green ball went into the corner pocket. She hooted, shifted, then bent over the table again.

Max swore he could hear the reply of silent "hoots" from all the men there. All the bar stools were turned to face the pool table. Actually, he thought he heard some sighs and groans from along the crowded bar as the little red leather skirt eased its way up her thighs. Higher, higher...

For cripes sakes! He hoped she was at least wearing panties.

Someone stepped behind her, placed a hand on her hip, and leaned over her. Seemingly to give her some good advice. *Shit.* Like she needed advice; she had been doing well enough on her own. Everybody in the bar could see that!

Max slammed the now empty beer bottle on the bar behind him and let out a curse. Marc glanced at him sideways. The knowing look he got from his brother made him even more annoyed.

He watched as Amanda took the advice with a smile on her lips. She must have made a funny comment because the "helpful" man laughed—a little too loudly—in response.

Amanda missed the shot. So much for the help.

Max watched Amanda tactfully slip away from the guy's big, assertive paws.

Marc hastily rose from his stool to step in front of Max, effectively blocking his view. "Brother, don't do anything stupid. You have been drinking, and the last thing you want is to lose your job." Marc waited until his brother looked at him. Not without obvious impatience. "And you...*we* are the law in this town. We must lead by example, not get into bar fights. It's not worth it."

Max grunted in response as he snagged the fresh beer the bartender slid in front of him. He pushed around his brother and stepped over to the pool table. Amanda was leaning on her pool stick, watching her new acquaintance take a shot.

"Who's your friend?"

Amanda lifted her shoulders slightly. She looked over at her opponent sideways. "What was your name?"

A hurt expression flashed over the guy's features before he answered, "Jack."

Amanda turned back to Max and repeated, "Jack."

"Known him long?"

"Oh, about," she glanced at the neon-trimmed Budweiser clock that hung above the bar, "an hour?"

Max turned his attention to Jack. "Where ya from, Jack?"

"Parsington."

"Parsington?" No wonder he didn't know the guy. He knew everyone in town; that was his job. "What are you doing here?"

Jack slowly and carefully laid the cue stick on the table and turned to give Max his full concentration. "Last thing I heard was this here was a free country."

Max leaned close to Jack, getting in his face. "Listen, Jack—"

An abrupt clearing of a throat made him realize he was royally fucking up right now. He straightened and backed up a step. But he kept his eyes narrowed and focused on the man in front of him.

Jack put his palms up in front of his chest and backed up a step. "Hey, I haven't done anything wrong. It is perfectly legal to have a drink with a pretty lady."

Amanda stepped between them, glaring at Max. "You're right, Jack. It isn't illegal to have a drink with a woman—and thank you for the compliment." She gave the other man a big smile, then turned back to Max.

"Can I have a word with you?" When Max hesitated, she added firmly, "Like right now?" She tilted her head toward a quiet corner in the dimly lit bar.

When she walked away, Max had no doubt that he was to follow her. No matter what. No ifs, ands, or buts about it.

He watched her tight, supple ass sway in that short skirt as she walked with determination. And he was sure he wasn't the only one appreciating the view. He didn't even want to turn his head to confirm it. He was trying to control his temper enough already.

In a darkened corner of the room, she leaned against the old wood paneling and crossed her arms over her chest to face him. "So—"

"Why didn't you tell me that you were going out tonight?"

Her eyebrows almost rose to her hairline before they dropped and her lips pressed flat.

He was on thin ice. But never before had he been so possessive of a woman he'd only slept with once. Once!

Why? What was it about this little slip of a woman that made him want to throw her over his shoulder, beat feet out of this bar, and take her home to throw her on his bed?

He wanted to fuck her on a real bed. Not in the backseat of a car. Not in his truck. But a bed where he could spread her out and do to her what needed to be done, so—

"Remember what you told me? We were supposed to be keeping this on the DL so your mommy didn't find out?"

Did he say that? *Damn.* "Yeah, but..."

"Nothing serious, right?"

Max bounced his fist off his forehead and frowned. "Right."

"So now you want me to check in with you before I go out?" Her brows shot up.

Yes. *Yes, I need to know where you are at all times and with whom. Damn it.* "No."

She nodded her head. "Good, because it would be a damn shame to have someone want to control my life in all aspects, wouldn't it?"

Max brushed his fingers over his short hair. She was playing him. She was throwing his words back at him, being a complete smart-ass. And enjoying every second.

But it didn't matter that she might not have come here to the bar with him tonight; she was damn sure going to end up in his bed tonight and not with someone like Jack from Parsington. Not if he had anything to say about it.

Without waiting for an answer, she pushed herself away from the wall and approached Marc at the bar. His brother was shaking his head and chuckling.

She paused in front of Marc. "You tell your brother he needs to be at my house in ten minutes or I'm not letting him in."

Max sighed as she headed out of the bar, tossing back her hair. Marc yelled out to her, "Happy New Year!" with a bark of laughter.

To Max, he asked, "What are you waiting for, fool?"

AMANDA QUIETLY OPENED the front door; she didn't want to wake Greg. She placed the car keys on the table as she walked into the room. She dug out some cash before throwing her purse into the nearby brown recliner and kicking off her heels.

Greg's sitter was nodding off in front of the television in the sunroom. With a gentle shake, Amanda woke Joni and saw the girl to the door, giving her the money and her thanks. She shut the door and leaned against it, letting out a ragged breath.

Okay, the man was hot, and there was definitely attraction—at least sexually—between them, but he was a bossy cop who couldn't mind his own damn business. She didn't think casual sex was his thing. He seemed way too possessive for that.

A slight tap on the door startled her. She peeked through the curtain covering the door's window. He'd come.

She stilled. Maybe it wasn't such a good idea that she'd invited him over. She could pretend she hadn't heard it and just go to bed. Or she could...

"Amanda, I see you standing there," she heard muffled through the door. Well, she could still ignore him and go to bed. Just because he was a cop didn't mean he could enter her house whenever he wanted. He would need some sort of search warrant. Wouldn't he?

Oh hell. He had entered this house plenty of times before without asking.

The door handle jiggled. "Amanda," he called in a fierce whisper. "Come on, let me in."

"Why should I?" She stepped over to the door, shifting the curtain aside to look out at him. Yes, he definitely was hot. *Shit.*

"Because you invited me."

Oh yeah. There was that.

"It didn't take you long." She opened the door before she could stop herself, and he walked in, filling the room with the scent of his maleness.

"You said ten minutes, and I didn't want you to change your mind."

But at that moment her need to put him in his place was stronger than her desire. "I was having an innocent game of pool. As *if* it was any of your business. What gives you the right to interfere with my night out? I was trying to have some fun in this disgustingly dull town."

Max scrubbed a hand over his prickly short hair, his irritation clearly showing on his face. "That was hardly innocent. Your *business* was hanging out of that short skirt of yours." He eyed the skirt, sending a wave of heat through her.

Amanda pursed her lips and planted a hand on her hip. "Maybe I was. Maybe I wanted to take Jack home and have hot, furious, sweaty sex with him. You know, like a casual wham-bam-thank-you-ma'am type of thing."

Max paused, and Amanda watched his Adam's apple bounce a couple times before he blurted, "Well, if you're looking for volunteers..."

"Are you applying?"

"Maybe." Max grabbed her arm to pull her close. "Damn, you're really hot when you're angry."

Amanda pulled away from him and went over to the nearby secretary's desk. She grabbed a sheet of notepaper and a pen. She shoved them into his chest.

"Here, fill out an application. I'll call you when I'm interviewing." She turned sharply, heading into the kitchen. He followed her and tossed the pen and paper onto the kitchen table. She crossed her arms and leaned back against the counter.

"Amanda..."

Amanda raised one hand to stop him from nearing. She needed to set some ground rules first. "You're not my keeper."

"I know."

"I'm not your business."

He paused, slightly longer than he should have, before answering. "I know."

"You're only agreeing with me to appease me." If he answered her with an *I know* again, she was going to kick him where it hurt.

Amanda headed toward the sunroom.

"That's right, walk away like the little girl that you are."

Amanda stopped in her tracks.

That son of a bitch! She spun and headed right back to him. She stood five-three looking up at his six-two.

With a muttered curse, she reached up, grabbed his shirt collar, and pulled his head to her. As her lips raked his, she could feel his surprise. His mouth parted, allowing her to shove her tongue between his lips.

Their tongues mated and fought; he angled his head to get even closer. His hands came up to grab her hips. Flushed and out of breath, Amanda stepped back with a calculated look. She unbuttoned her ivory blouse. Slowly. Releasing one shiny button from its prison, then another. Until her blouse hung open, exposing her tan, tight abdomen and her gold belly ring. His eyes raked her black, lacy bra and the rounded flesh above it. Her nipples hardened. Her breath caught.

Amanda slipped the smooth fabric over her shoulders, and with a shrug her blouse slid to the floor.

She reached up to touch the front clasp that barely kept her breasts in check.

"Amanda," he warned again, but could only manage to suck in a breath when her fingers released the clasp and her full breasts escaped. "Jesus!"

"So, Officer Bryson, am," her voice caught, "am I a little girl?"

Max's eyes gleamed darkly as he raised them from her chest to her face. His jaw clenched and unclenched. "No." His nostrils flared as if he were fighting a demon inside. "Hell, no."

With a throaty laugh, she pulled off the bra, dropping it to the floor with her discarded blouse. Lifting a hand to her throat, she trailed a finger down her chest to circle one of her painfully hard nipples. She crossed over to circle the other one. She bit her lip and threw her head back, her eyelids lowered. Amanda's breathing deepened as she slid her hand over her flat belly and circled a red fingernail around her gold belly ring. Then she went lower.

Max was still. So still. Too still. She wanted him. Wanted him to take her. Here. Now. Why wasn't he moving?

"Fuck," she groaned. Continuing a path downward, she popped open the snap on her skirt; then the slide of the zipper sounded deafening.

She flicked her tongue over parted lips, leaving a trail of moisture. She was panting ever so slightly.

Max's eyes had followed every move. He had been glued in place. Until now...

He grabbed her by the waist, lifted her up, turned around, and practically tossed her onto the counter. Grabbing her waistband, he ripped her skirt down over her hips, taking her thong underwear with it in one handful.

Amanda said nothing. Their words always seemed to ruin the moment. She didn't want that. She wanted his body against hers, his weight crushing her, his lips on every part of her. She needed his tongue to dip into every crevice.

She wanted to scream a mindless scream as she orgasmed over and over.

And she wasn't disappointed.

One second he was looming above her, and in the next, he was down on his knees, spreading her thighs, looking closer.

Then he took her in his mouth. He flicked her clit with his tongue once, twice, before stroking it. Amanda dropped her head back against the cabinet and let out a low wail. She blindly reached for him, grabbing the back of his head, pulling him closer, if that was possible.

His fingers separated her heat, stroking along with his tongue, tasting, nipping. Just teasing, teasing until her inner muscles clenched with need.

He dipped his tongue into her, torturing her. He was torturing her! His fingers replaced his tongue, thrusting deep as his lips captured her clit once more. He suckled as his fingers found a rhythm.

She forced herself to swallow her scream; she didn't want to wake Greg. She didn't want him wandering downstairs to find his sister spread-eagle on the counter while the local cop was treating her like a smorgasbord.

Her thoughts evaporated as his thumb replaced his mouth on her clit and he stood. But his lips clamped on her nipple and his free hand found her other breast. He pinched her nipple, twisted it enough to make her arch her back. His teeth scraped the other over and over; then his tongue would soothe away the sting.

She let out a soft gasp, then a low wail as she felt the orgasm start. Her muscles exploded into furious contractions around his fingers. Max stiffened and paused. He lifted his head and looked at her.

"Holy shit," was all he said before he took her mouth, plundering her, thrusting his fingers in her, starting the pleasure all over again. She tasted herself on his lips and she almost came again, but he pulled away.

In what seemed like a split second, Max was standing naked before her. Beautiful. A dark stud. His cock was so hard, so erect it looked almost agonizing. The head held a pearly drop of precum. She wanted to lick it off.

She pulled her gaze away to meet his; his eyes pinned her with intensity. So intense she felt a flicker of fear, but it was washed away when he grabbed her hips and thrust deep into her, filling her up, stretching her.

Her gasp made him pause, his chest rising and falling rapidly. She thrust her hips against him, wanting more, wanting him deeper and harder, but he held her still. "Don't. Don't move... just for a second." Then he gritted his teeth and thrust deeply again and again.

She wrapped her legs tightly around his waist. She met each thrust with a thrust of her own. She ground herself against him, wanting every inch of his cock.

His arms were planted on either side of her on the counter, shaking. He was struggling with his own control. He kissed her again, his tongue briefly tangling with hers before he had to pull away, to catch his breath. His jaw tightened as his hips tilted with each thrust. He pounded her hard. He wanted this. She wanted this. There was no need to get romantic. No frills. Just want. Just need.

She arched her back, and as she came again, she sank her teeth into his shoulder to control her screams.

A bead of sweat rolled off him to mingle with hers. He reached up and grabbed her hair, pulling it back roughly, exposing her neck to him. And he sank his teeth into her throat, not breaking skin but hard enough to make her shudder and her pussy muscles tightened on him even more.

She moaned—she had no idea what. Nor did she care because he tensed and was coming deep within her. Her body pumped him dry. He collapsed on her, his face buried into her neck.

Their breathing was fast and deep, his heart pounding against her.

Max pulled his hands from beneath her and intertwined his fingers with hers. He still had her pinned on the countertop. He brushed a light kiss against her neck where his head laid.

Amanda couldn't move. Not that she wanted to. He was still inside her, stretching her. She didn't want to lose that closeness. At least, not yet.

Besides interlocking their hands, Max had hardly moved either. Then he lifted his head to look deep into her eyes. She wanted him to say something profound. That he loved her. That he couldn't live without her. Anything!

"Holy shit." He brushed his lips lightly over hers. "That was un-fucking-believable."

Well, maybe not anything. Even though he wasn't the only one that wanted casual sex, why did it bother her when he acted as such? As Amanda squirmed, he withdrew and stood. He held out a hand and pulled her up. She sat on the counter, naked as a newborn, looking at the man she'd just given herself to.

"Yeah, that was un-fucking-believable," she mimicked.

Max brushed her wild, damp auburn curls out of her face and tucked them behind her ear. He ran a thumb along her jawline and then planted another kiss on her lips.

All of a sudden the kitchen lights seemed glaringly harsh to Amanda. She quickly became self-conscious. Well, she should. She was sitting buck naked on the kitchen counter just having had wild sex with a cop.

Damn. She pushed herself off the smooth counter and gathered her clothes. She made a mental note to bleach the counter in the morning.

Hell, she should just have them replaced.

"Amanda, will you go out with me?"

She stopped dead and gave him an incredulous look. "What?"

He was getting dressed and had just buttoned his jeans. His bare chest was still damp. Dark hair circled his navel and disappeared deep into the denim. He looked so edible.

Damn. Quit it. That's what had gotten her in trouble in the first place.

"Seriously, I want to take you out." Max bent over to pick up his shirt. "Like on a date."

Wait. Now he was asking her on a date? So... this wasn't as casual as either of them had planned?

A real date. Like out in public? To hell with his mother finding out?

She pursed her lips and squinted. Was it her that was confused or was it him?

Ah fuck. Did she even really care at this moment?

The flexing of his bicep with the Marine *Semper Fi* tattoo caught her attention as he slipped into his shirt. Once it was hidden from view, she responded, "I don't know if I can trust you on a date. You might try to take advantage of me."

Max let out a low chuckle, making Amanda's heart skip a beat. One of Greg's favorite words popped into her head —*yummy*. Max was so yummy.

"Look, bring Greg along. We'll have fun." He grabbed her hips and held her close. Max dropped his head to hers and placed a kiss on her lips. He deepened it before letting her go. "I'll pick you and Greg up tomorrow night. Say yes."

No, no, no.

"Yes."

Chapter Ten

MAX HAD RENTED the old type of skates for Greg and Rollerblades for himself and Amanda. She watched Max out of the corner of her eye. So much for going to the bar last night to get him off her mind. That plan had completely backfired. Well, there had been one high point of the night.

Currently it was an "All Skate" and there were quite a few people on the floor going in circles. Max had Greg in the center, out of the way of traffic, working on his balance. Greg shuffled along, holding on to Max's outstretched arm with both hands. A huge smile covered his face. He loved the attention he was receiving from the cop.

Well, at least *someone* was getting attention.

Amanda was becoming bored rollerblading in a circle. She preferred rollerblading along Florida's beaches, like at the famous Broadwalk, where there was sun and fun.

In this godforsaken place there wasn't sun *or* fun. All right, she was being a little *too* harsh.

She skated to the side, deciding to watch some of Manning

Grove's young residents do their thing—skate and socialize. She couldn't imagine that the kids liked the music. It was so lame.

A guy about Greg's age skated up, skidding to a stop inches from her, attempting to impress. "Hi!"

"Hello," she responded, watching a huge grin cross his face.

He looked her up and down—not *real* obvious—and puffed out his chest. "I'm Toby."

He was young and not bad looking. However, immaturity just oozed from his pores. He reminded her of a hot-blooded Latino she had left back in Miami.

Amanda realized he was still waiting for a response. "Oh, I'm Amanda."

The lights dimmed, and a sappy love song blared from the ancient speakers. It was a "Couples Only" skate.

"Wanna?"

Amanda looked at Toby's offered hand and tried not to laugh. But at that same moment the hairs on the back of her neck stood up. Across the rink another man's icy blue eyes had her in his crosshairs.

Officer Bryson's recurrent warnings of "stay out of trouble" bounced around in her brain. And for once, she figured she'd try to heed his advice.

"No thanks."

"You're pretty."

Amanda rolled her eyes. *Jeez*, his lines were as lame as the music. "Thanks."

"You're new around here." It was more of a statement than a question, and Amanda didn't bother to respond. "You got a boyfriend?"

Amanda opened her mouth—she was going to say no or she wasn't looking or that he was too young for her or point out that there were a lot of nice girls closer to his own age. But she never got the chance.

Instead Toby let out an "oomph" as Max *accidentally* ran into him.

"Oh, sorry, Toby. Are you okay?"

Toby appeared a bit miffed, but looked up at the larger man and begrudgingly said, "Yes, sir."

"Do you mind if I skate with my date?"

"No, go ahead, Officer Bryson. As long as Amanda doesn't mind."

Wimp.

Max reached out, snagged her hand, and pulled her away. "Nah, she doesn't mind."

As soon as they were a few feet away, Max asked, "Making friends?"

"Yes."

"He's a bit young."

"And your point is?"

"I'd think after last night you'd prefer a man over a little boy."

Amanda made sure he saw the eye roll. "Sure, if I *knew* one." Amanda looked around. "Where's Greg?"

"I gave him some quarters. He's in the arcade."

"Oh." They did another circle around the rink as the disco ball bounced colorful reflections off walls and floor. "We better go check on him."

"He's fine. Dunn's here with his baby sister. They're keeping him busy."

They skated a couple more loops in silence. His warm fingers interlocked with hers. It wouldn't have been a big deal, except that the thumb he kept rubbing over the back of her hand was sending shivers up her spine.

Max skated to a stop in a dark corner and faced her, staring deep into her eyes.

He was crazy. One hundred percent certifiably crazy.

She was the cause.

He had become a jealous asshole. He lowered himself to nothing more than a caveman anytime another man spoke to, touched, or even looked cross-eyed at Amanda.

This wasn't him. He had never in his life been so possessive of a female. He was a catch. He knew that; his mother told him so. He was deeply respected in this town. He was a good cop. He was financially stable and he was decent looking. He could have his choice of any single woman in this town. Well, just about.

But, he didn't want just any woman.

He wanted Amanda.

He brushed her wild hair away from her face. He ran a thumb over her plump bottom lip.

She was driving him nuts. His testosterone was in overdrive. Her pink tongue slipped out to taste his thumb, causing his groin to tighten.

His voice was uneven as he said, "I know that this is only our first official date, but can I get a kiss?"

Her eyes widened, then narrowed as she studied his face. "I don't know. I don't want you to think I'm easy."

He chuckled. "Too late."

Instead of complying, she rolled backward, leaving a gap between them. She planted her hands on her hips. "Hmm. I guess I will have to play hard to get now."

Amanda inched backward every time Max inched forward. "I know how to play hard. You want to see hard?"

The lights went up, and the song changed to an old disco tune. Amanda skated away, flinging her hair back as she gave him a look over her shoulder. The look held the promise of what was to come. Her lips tilted up at the corners, and she winked at him. Max pushed off the wall, rolling after her.

When he caught up with her on the other side of the rink, Max put his hands over her hips and rolled up tight behind her.

Amanda pushed her ass against him, swinging her hips to the beat of Donna Summer's "Love to Love You, Baby."

She circled her arms behind his neck, pushing her breasts out as she started to sing the lyrics. Amanda turned in his arms, her hands still looped around his neck, and she made a face like she was climaxing as she sang the last "Uh, love to love you, baby."

Holy fuck. They needed to go right now. Like *right* now. Though her singing sucked, his cock was so hard. It was twisted all up in his pants. And this skating rink was the last place he was going to adjust his raging hard-on.

"We need to get the hell out of here now. Let's go get Greg."

"Was it something I said?" she asked, her face now the look of innocence.

"Uh-huh. And I expect to hear the same thing a little later." *Just don't sing it.*

They collected Greg, turned in their skates, and were home within twenty minutes.

Max waited down in the living room while Amanda got Greg into his PJ's and turned on the TV in his room. He could hear the low sound of the TV show but nothing else. And he waited. And waited.

Maybe he should leave. Maybe she had been playing with him back at the skating rink just to get under his skin. He felt like a desperate fool standing here waiting. He turned but stopped when he heard her feet padding down the steps.

He did a double take since she came down wearing a frumpy, bulky robe.

"Why—"

"Shh." She grabbed his hand and pulled him toward the garage. "Just come with me."

He raised his eyebrows but tagged along as she pulled him through the garage door and shut it behind him. It had a double key deadbolt, and she turned the key, locking them in.

"What—"

"Shh." She led him to the back of the Buick and opened the rear passenger-side door. "Get in."

"But—"

"Shh. Get in."

He released her hand and slid into the backseat. She slid in after him and shut the door.

She turned to him, and their faces were inches apart. "Now..."

"Now..."

"Now we both shut up, since talking isn't our strongpoint, and you finish what you started in this car on Christmas night."

Even in the dim light, he could see her naughty grin. *Damn.* She continually surprised him.

Naughty, naughty girl. He loved it.

He fought back a smile and asked, "Do you remember what I was doing to you?"

"Shh. No talking. Don't screw this up."

"Just screw you?"

He reached out and cupped her face, tilted her head, pulled her a little closer. He leaned in and kissed her, sucking in her lower lip. His tongue tangled with hers, and her hands grabbed his biceps. His muscles tightened and he pulled back, just enough to pull his long-sleeve T-shirt over his head.

He caught her reaction. She wanted him. Knowing that, seeing that, made his cock rock hard, his balls tight. He wanted her just as much. No, more.

"Amanda—"

She shut him up by pressing her lips to his again, making him swallow his words.

That's right. No talking. Just action. She was a bossy little thing.

He moved until he was sucking on her earlobe, flicking her earring with his tongue. Then nipped her tender skin. He moved down her neck, nipping at her collarbone, pushing away the collar of the robe. Feeling for the belt, he released it. He couldn't wait to see what she was wearing.

She slid the robe off her shoulders and showed him exactly what she wasn't wearing. She was 100 percent, bona fide naked under that thing. All skin and flesh and those glorious breasts.

They were perfect. Hard nipples surrounded by soft flesh. He cupped both of them, circling his thumbs over her areolae. Once, twice. She arched her back and closed her eyes. He took one nipple into his mouth and sucked deeply. When a moan escaped her, his cock tried to do a dance in his jeans, but they were too tight. A prison. He needed to get out of them and quick.

He popped the snap on his jeans, but before he could go farther, her hands pushed his away, so he went back to "appreciating" her breasts. Stroking, pinching, twisting her nipples as she worked his zipper down.

"Take them off." Her words came breathlessly and he looked at her. Her eyes were hooded and unfocused, her mouth slightly open. "Hurry."

He pulled away, lifted his hips, and shoved his jeans down as quickly as he could. He kicked off his shoes and socks before removing the jeans completely. His cock was free. And throbbing. He wanted to stroke it, but Amanda beat him to it. Her hand encased him and she squeezed gently, her thumb wiping a drop of precum off the head.

Holy shit. Holy shit! He felt like an inexperienced eighteen-year-old. Like he could blow any second.

There was no way in hell he was going to allow that to happen. No way.

But this was what she did to him. And he needed to stay in control so she wouldn't regret this decision.

"I'm so hard."

Amanda leaned over, her lips just brushing the head. She looked up at him briefly, a wicked smile on her face.

What a freaking vixen.

She took him into her warm, wet mouth. And he cried out. His breathing quickened and he tried to swallow. Her tongue swirled along the edge of the crown of his cock. Teasing. Then she took his length in her mouth, stroking him again and again.

He wanted to pleasure her. Touch her. Kiss her. But he was frozen fast. He couldn't move. She had to stop. Like soon. Like... like now!

With a groan, he shifted away from her, breaking her contact.

Another shift and he was using his chest to push her back along the seat. Grabbing her knees, he spread her as wide as the car allowed. He dived in, his mouth on her wet heat.

It was her turn to cry out as he sucked her clit, flicked her with his tongue. She tasted so good. He slid two fingers into her, and he could feel her clamping down, squeezing, while lifting her hips. He kept licking and sucking her tender spot as she rode his fingers in a frantic rhythm. Her head dropped back, her body bowing. She screamed, "I'm coming!"

More wet heat as she throbbed around his fingers. Before she could catch her breath, he shifted one last time, sliding into her. She was tight but wet. So wet. Her body welcomed him, matching him stroke for stroke. The tilt of her hips met the tilt of his perfectly. They fit perfectly.

Max gritted his teeth, not wanting to lose it. He wanted this to continue as long as he could. He pulled out of her, and she released a small whimper.

He sat up and pulled her with him, her legs straddling him.

He looked into her face and saw the raw desire there. A drip of sweat landed on her breast, and he captured it between his lips.

He held her hips tightly, so she couldn't lower herself. Not yet. She struggled against him.

He suckled her nipples, first one and the other, keeping her suspended above him. A flush ran up her chest as she struggled. He nipped both nipples one more time before releasing his hold on her hips. She slid down and settled onto him. Her forehead dropped to his chest, her breathing heavy and uneven against his skin.

He was so deep. Her riding him buried his cock base to tip. He was afraid to move. He was right on the edge.

She circled her hips just a little.

She was playing with fire.

With her on top, she had all the power. But he didn't care. He slapped her ass and she began to move. Riding him hard.

She had complete control, her rhythm, her movements. Her release.

He could feel she was close, her pussy tightening around him. She released small sounds that drove him nuts. Made him want to thrust up hard. Again and again until he came.

He closed his eyes and tried to slow his breathing. Sweat trickled down his face. He was so done. So, so done. His cock was so hard that it almost hurt. His balls were tight, so ready to release.

Amanda tensed and screamed. Her pussy pulsated around him, and that was all it took. He let go and screamed with her, one last push deep inside her.

They both collapsed within each other's arms. The only sound was their shaky, harsh breathing.

He caught his breath enough to say, "Amanda..."

Amanda had her eyes closed and was collapsed against him, still in his lap. She put one finger up to his lips.

"Don't. Don't fuck this up."

TEDDY LOOKED up from the brush he was cleaning as Amanda entered the salon. "Hey, girlfriend, go ahead and put that luscious rump of yours in the chair."

She went over to the nearest station and plopped herself into the black vinyl seat. She spun it around to look at herself in the mirror. She looked the same, didn't she?

Teddy came up behind her and automatically snapped the plastic cape around her neck. Amanda's gaze met his in the glass.

"You're too quiet." Teddy's teeth gnawed on his bottom lip. She could see the wheels turning in his head.

Oh shit.

"Okay, spill the beans. What's up with you?"

"Nothing." She attempted to distract him with, "Just take the ends off."

Teddy spun the chair around, stopping it abruptly with his foot when they were face-to-face. Her neck snapped from the force.

"Uh-uh. There will be no taking any ends off until I hear some dirt."

"There's *nothing*." She emphasized the last word.

"*Hmph*. Girl, there is *something*..."

"What are you, the newest detective for the Manning Grove PD?" Her voice trailed off as she realized that she'd just given him a clue.

His lips formed a big O, and his eyes widened. "You didn't."

Amanda grimaced at his high-pitched screech.

"Oh no, you didn't!" He spun her around again and reclined the chair back in one swoop, then began to wash her hair. "I want to hear every detail."

"No."

"Please?"

"No."

"It was that Bryson buck, wasn't it?"

Amanda wanted to ignore him, but she couldn't. Her head was in a sink and Teddy's face hovered six inches above her, staring her down. It was a bloody inquisition.

Teddy rinsed her hair, sighing dreamily. "It was! *Mmm. Mmm. Mmm.*" He yanked her up and rubbed her head with a towel. "Max 'I'm So Hot I Sizzle When I Walk' Bryson?"

"Teddy!"

"C'mon. Give a poor, lonely guy a bone." He giggled at his own words. "Was it good?"

"It was great," she conceded.

"Then why aren't you happy? Why aren't you just exploding with joy?"

"I don't know."

"You have great sex—it had to be; don't tell me it wasn't—and you sit there moping?"

"It's more complicated than that."

Teddy put a hand to his mouth to cover a drama-queen gasp. "Oh my Lord." Teddy whipped the chair around and leaned down to look her straight in the eyes. "Yep. You're in love."

Amanda paled. Love? No. Lust, maybe. The sex was good. That was it.

"It's hardly love, Teddy. Hell, we've only been on one official date. And even Greg was along on that."

"But you've had carnal knowledge of him, right? Don't tell me you haven't."

Amanda reluctantly nodded her head, her cheeks on fire.

"Ooooo, so it was hot and furious? I'm so jealous."

"But, honestly, I don't get it. One minute we want to jump each other's bones and then the next... Sometimes he just confuses me. The problem is that he's always in my business, and I don't want that in a man. I had enough of that with my mother."

"Honey, he's a damn cop. He can't help but be bossy and controlling. You know that saying, there's a fine line between love and hate."

That line was like a tightrope that Max and she were walking. One little bobble and—

"So, did you have fun the other night at Crazy Pete's? Were you disappointed? You know, we ought to start up a big flaming gay bar with lots of great music and dancing and lights... Ooooh, the thought. We'd see how many of the locals come out of the closet. You could bartend and I'd—"

Teddy continued to chitchat, his lips moving a mile a minute. Amanda had no idea what he was saying.

Chapter Eleven

Amanda awoke and stretched. It was Thursday, one of the days Greg didn't go to day care. She thought of the pancake mix she had purchased the other day along with the fresh strawberries. It was going to be her first attempt at making pancakes. The microwavable ones didn't count.

She dragged a brush through her long hair, tugging at knots with her fingers. After five minutes, she relented and tossed the brush back onto the dresser. She'd get her hair back in order once she washed it later. She straightened out her pink-striped pajama bottoms and made sure her little white tank top covered all the important stuff before heading down the hallway to Greg's room.

His door was ajar. A sick feeling in the pit of her stomach hit her. She pushed it open wider. "Greg?"

She groaned as she ran down the stairs. Chaos ran up to meet her halfway. At least the dog was here. That was a good sign.

"Where's he at, Chaos?" The dog barked in response. Amanda let out a curse. What did she expect, the dog to act like Lassie and lead her to Greg?

Hell yes, she did.

"C'mon, Chaos. Where's he at?"

The dog barked and rushed down the steps beside her. At the bottom he circled twice, let out a shrill bark, and scampered to the front door.

She jammed the heel of her hand into her forehead. He was gone. Again.

"He went out the front door?" she asked the dog. Chaos barked once more and spun.

Shit! She was having a freaking conversation with a dog!

Amanda ran into the family room, snatched up the phone, and dialed 911.

"9-1-1. What's your emergency?"

"My brother! He's missing!"

"Okay, ma'am. Calm down. Your brother is missing?"

Didn't she just say that? "Yes!"

"How long has he been missing for?"

"I don't know. An hour?"

A silent pause. "How old is he?"

"Twenty-two."

Another slight pause. "Ma'am, he is an adult. Call us back after—"

"But he's...he's...not right!" Amanda slammed the phone down. "Damn it!"

She bit her lip, drawing blood. She tried to think, but her head was spinning.

This was not supposed to be happening. They were supposed to be eating a nice breakfast of pancakes and syrup.

She grabbed the car keys off the hook.

She'd have to find Greg herself.

"Let's go, boy!"

RED, white, and blue lights flashed behind her, illuminating the inside of the car like a bad disco.

She cursed and slammed the steering wheel. Just what she needed.

As she opened the driver's side window, Max's head was suddenly filling the window. It was déjà vu.

"Amanda. What the hell are you doing? You ran through a red light. You're going to get yourself killed."

"Well, maybe this is the only way to get police help!"

"What?"

"I called 911, but they wouldn't help."

"What's wrong?"

"Greg. He's missing."

"Christ! Again?"

Again? Yes, again. She had failed once again. She'd proved to herself and to Max Bryson that she was irresponsible. Once again.

Clasping both hands tightly on the steering wheel, she bit her lip to keep back the sob that so wanted to escape. "I'm so sorry." She closed her eyes.

"It's not me you have to apologize to." He reached up to his shoulder and got on the radio, giving Greg's description to his dispatcher. "Now go home. You've got to be there if he comes home. Call me if he does. I'll have the guys out looking for him."

Max reached into the window and ran his thumb down her cheek, brushing away a stray tear. His voice was low, soft. "He'll be fine."

He sounded so convincing.

She didn't go home. She couldn't.

There was no way she was going home to sit and worry. After Max had sent her on her way, she drove around town once more. Then parked. Chaos ran circles around her, the border collie herding her down the sidewalk. She checked the Fifth Street Church. Greg wasn't there.

Out front, she sat down on the bone-jarringly cold stone steps. She shivered uncontrollably. She should have thrown on her jacket. And a pair of shoes. She was running around town in the middle of winter with nothing on but pajamas. What was she thinking?

She wasn't! That was the problem. But she needed clear thoughts.

Greg was most likely looking for his mother. But he wasn't at the church. Where would he look next? Think!

The last time Greg saw his mother was at the church.

Amanda straightened. But it wasn't. Really, the last time Greg saw his mother was... the cemetery! The cemetery was three blocks away.

She ran, mindless of the dog that nipped at her heels. She ran, not even caring that her bare feet pounded mercilessly into the concrete. She ran until she saw the cemetery.

Until she saw them.

Two cruisers, their lights spinning, were parked nose to nose. One had its driver's door hanging open. Both were empty.

Relief overwhelmed Amanda at the sight of two familiar broad-shouldered men in dark blue patrol jackets as they flanked Greg, talking to him just a few feet within the cemetery gates.

He was safe. Greg was safe. She called out in relief. All three men looked up.

Suddenly she realized she must look silly. Still in her pink pajamas and white tank. Without a jacket in the cold weather. And barefoot! She stopped on the sidewalk, looking at them across the street.

Then Greg spotted Chaos. And the border collie caught sight of Greg. The dog's ears pricked and he barked. Greg's smile widened and he automatically patted his leg. Chaos responded. His eyes were only for his master.

It was something Amanda would never forget, burned in her brain forever.

A honk. A squeal. A thud.

A sickening thud.

Sounds Amanda would never want to hear again in her life.

"Chaos!" Frozen in time, horror engulfed her. Her head shook in slow motion. She screamed silently, sounds fighting to escape.

She barely heard a horn blare as she stepped off the curb. Suddenly she was caught up in strong, thick arms. The arms wrapped around her tightly, causing her to fight violently against the restraint. She found her voice and screamed hysterically, "No! No! No! Chaos!"

Max's face brushed against hers, and he whispered soothing words into her ear. But she couldn't hear him. She couldn't see him. All she could see was the lifeless, black-and-white dog lying out in the road, his plumed tail still.

Amanda raised her eyes. Marc was holding Greg back. The look on Greg's face made her want to vomit. She doubled over in Max's arms, dry heaves racking her body.

She croaked, "Is he okay?" already knowing the answer.

People were gathering. Someone was picking up Chaos and wrapping him with a tan blanket. Then everything faded to black.

AMANDA FELT the light tapping of fingers against her cheek. She didn't want to open her eyes. She wasn't ready to deal with what was going on. Not yet. If she kept her eyes shut for a few more minutes...

"Amanda? Amanda, wake up."

She could feel the unbearable cold of the concrete seeping through the bones of her lower body. She was surrounded by Max's heat as he squatted, holding her upper body between his legs, supporting her.

He tapped her cheek again.

She felt his hot breath against her ear. "Damn it, Amanda. I know you've come to. Open your eyes. Or I'll get out the smelling salts."

She complied with a frown. She was lying on the sidewalk in the same spot where she had fainted. His body was blocking the view of the street.

"Greg?"

"Marc will get him over to my parents. My mother will take good care of him."

Mary Ann. What would Amanda do without her?

"Can you stand now?"

Amanda nodded. "I think so."

Max hooked his arms under hers and lifted her to her feet. He wrapped a silver Mylar blanket tightly around her. When she tried to peek around him to the street, he grabbed her shoulders, then reached up to lift her chin. He looked down at her as if peering deep into her soul. Amanda folded her arms across her stomach and pressed against the emptiness she felt there.

"Are you okay to drive?" Max asked.

She nodded wordlessly.

"Are you sure?"

"I'm not sure about anything right now."

"Go home and rest until I get there. We'll take care of Chaos." He stopped her. "And Amanda?"

Lifeless, she stared at him.

"This time listen. Go home."

She closed her eyes for a moment and, after giving him a

slight nod, began the three-block walk back to the Buick. She tightened the emergency blanket around her shivering body and refused to look back.

MAX WATCHED Amanda walk away down the street. Her gait was stiff as if in a lot of pain. She was barefoot. In January.

The little fool.

He should have offered her a ride back to the car, but right now he was feeling anything but generous.

Well, she wasn't the only one hurting. He couldn't get the picture of Greg out of his mind—how he saw his beloved dog almost killed right in front of his eyes. It shouldn't have happened like this.

Hell, this shouldn't have happened at all.

Here Greg was—still looking for his mother because he couldn't understand her death. And now his companion had been seriously hurt...hell, almost fatally injured. Max didn't know if Greg even understood the concept of loss, of death.

Hopefully Max's mother could soothe him, calm him down, and get Greg's mind off the tragedy that just happened.

Amanda, in her current emotional state, would be no help to her brother right now.

Damn her.

Damn her! How could she be so foolish?

He had told her to *go home and wait.*

Max crossed the street to where Marc was standing with an arm around a frantic Greg. After Marc settled Greg into the back of his cruiser, his brother had told him that, when Max had been busy with Amanda, Dunn had taken off, code three, lights and sirens, to the nearest animal hospital with Chaos.

With a numb shake of his head, he sent Marc with Greg off to his parent's house. He sent the driver, who had narrowly missed Amanda, on his way also.

The other driver who hit the poor dog was waiting beside her vehicle, clearly shaken up. He took minimal information from the woman but checked to make sure that she was not injured and that there was no damage to the vehicle. He told her he would write up an incident report. He apologized for all the inconvenience, his voice sounding wooden and hollow.

He went through the motions of doing his duty, but the whole time he felt like he was being stuck with a hot poker in his gut.

The vision of Amanda almost stepping off the curb in front of that car was burned in his brain.

She could have been killed.

He held his hands out in front of him. They were still trembling. He made tight fists to control his weakness, and his mouth twisted grimly.

AMANDA BLINKED, trying to clear her head.

She had come straight home like Max told her to. She had drawn the shades to darken the bedroom. Then she had curled up in bed, closing her eyes, trying to keep out the world.

It didn't help.

The cool washcloth she had placed on her forehead earlier was now warm. She dropped it on the floor beside the bed in disgust. That hadn't helped either. The pounding in her head wasn't subsiding. She didn't think that a whole bottle of aspirin would even alleviate it.

Amanda heard a slight tap on her bedroom door.

She pushed herself up as Max stepped into the room, his unmistakably tense body filling the small space at the foot of her bed. His uniform gave him an air of authority and severity. And his expression was just plain unreadable.

She had expected to see concern, maybe even sadness, in his face. But his expression revealed nothing.

"Greg?"

"Unharmed but devastated." His words were tired.

"Chaos?" she asked hopefully.

"When I was dealing with you, Dunn showed up and rushed him to the vet. Last I heard he was in critical condition. We'll know more later after some tests and most likely some surgery."

She closed her eyes, trying to hold back the tears.

She was lucky that Chaos hadn't been killed instantly. And he was still critical; she was sure it could go either way at this point. Amanda hoped for Greg's sake he didn't lose his dog so soon after his mother.

"It was stupid. Stupid! I had told you to go home. *I told you to go home and wait.*" Anger wasn't even accurate; it was hurt and pain and fury. "But you didn't. You are a spoiled little brat that thinks you can do whatever you want. You don't have to listen to anyone. You could have gotten yourself killed. You could have gotten Greg killed, and you certainly got Chaos critically injured."

"I only wanted to help find Greg." Her voice trembled.

"When are you going to learn? Are you ever going to be responsible enough to care about anyone but yourself?"

His words hurt. But they were true. She was ashamed and sad. But mostly disappointed in herself.

She desperately fought her own anger that bubbled up. Anger at herself. Anger at the man who judged her from the end of her bed.

She lost the fight.

"I didn't want to come to this town in the first place. I want my life back!" She pulled her knees to her chest and hugged them tight. "I miss my life. I miss my friends. Heading out to Starbucks late at night or heading to the beach to work on my tan or hailing a taxi to head downtown to the shopping district to blow my rent. My life is now reduced to shopping at Kohl's. What happened? How did it get to this? I don't belong here!"

"Apparently." The lone word slashed her deeply.

"Get out," she screamed hysterically, her brain wanting to pound right out of her head. "Get the fuck out of my house!"

Her head pounded as she saw Max close his eyes and his whole body shudder. A mix of emotions crossed his face before he looked at her again. His eyes had softened, and the tightness in his body was gone.

"Amanda..."

No. No. No. She couldn't take his sympathy right now. If he softened, so would she, and she would only break into a million more pieces.

She needed to be alone right now.

"Just go," she whispered.

And he did.

MAX RUSHED DOWN THE STEPS, taking two at a time, the items on his bulky duty belt banging into his thighs and hips.

His nostrils flared as he sucked in deep breaths, trying to control his emotions. *Hell*, just trying to get back into some control at all. As a cop he dealt with these types of incidents practically every day. But this wasn't just any typical incident. This was Amanda. Watching her almost get hit by that car...

His heart felt as though it had been ripped out of his chest.

With heavy, long strides he walked through the small house and out the front door. He felt disappointment as he slammed the door behind him. Even though he had shut it hard enough to rattle the front windows, it hadn't given him any satisfaction, any relief in the pit of his stomach. He started for his patrol car but then abruptly turned and walked back to the stoop. He caught himself from going back inside and right back up those steps to her bedroom.

He wasn't going to do it. He wasn't going to give in.

He tightened his jaw. She needed some time. He needed some time. To process, to collect themselves.

He clenched his fists and began to pace back and forth on the front sidewalk.

He heard a rustle and looked over. Mrs. Myers was on her porch, leaning over the rail. Of course, watching him act like a fool.

"What's going on, Max?"

What the hell. Not now. Max gritted his teeth. "Nothing, Mrs. Myers. Why don't you go on back inside? It's a bit chilly out here. I wouldn't want you to get sick."

Mrs. Myers' fists plunked onto her meaty hips. "There always seems to be some sort of raucous going on over there. That girl has been nothing but trouble since she's come here. Someone needs to take that boy out of her care."

Max sighed. "She's doing the best that she can, Mrs. Myers."

It was true. She *was* doing the best she could. She wasn't perfect. Life wasn't clean and neat. Shit was always going to happen. But, damn... Today had just ripped him open and turned him inside out.

Marc rolled up in the other patrol car. He slid open the driver's side window as he pulled into the driveway.

"How's Greg?"

Marc shook his head, a look of sadness shadowing his features. "Not good. He's pretty distraught. Ma's doing what she can."

Max's lips pressed together, and he gave his brother a nod.

He glanced at his watch. "I'm going home now to change. I'll head over there as soon as I can and see what I can do."

"All right. See you tonight." Marc slowly drove away, giving Mrs. Myers a slight wave as he did so.

Mrs. Myers turned her attention back to Max. "What's wrong with the boy?"

"He's upset. His dog just got struck by a car."

"Can't say that's a shame, that noisy thing."

Max grunted and hopped into his car before he said something he'd regret.

AFTER SHOWERING AND CHANGING, Max headed over to his parents' house. Once he was sure that Greg was coping, he stepped out onto the porch to get some badly needed fresh air.

The rumble of tires on the gravel driveway made Max step over to the porch edge to see who was coming. He recognized the gray Buick.

He was determined to head Amanda off. His mother had finally calmed Greg down somewhat, and he didn't want all that work undone.

He jogged down the steps and over to the car, reaching Amanda just as she was climbing out. Max stepped in front of her, arms crossed and legs shoulder-width apart.

She wasn't happy to see him. Well, he wasn't so happy to see her over here so soon either. "What are you doing here?"

She pushed her sunglasses up enough to brush a frustrated hand over her eyes. He got enough of a glimpse to see they were puffy and red.

"I came to pick up Greg."

"That's not such a good idea right now."

She tried to step around him. "He needs me."

"If you want to help your brother, you'll let him spend the night here. My mother will take good care of him."

She paused. "But—"

"Let my parents distract him tonight, get his mind off everything that happened. My pop can drop him off tomorrow."

"He's got day care…" The sight of her biting her lip in indecision was tearing down his wall.

"I'll have him drop Greg off at day care tomorrow, if he's even up for it." He reached out, enveloping her hands within his, pulling her close. He dropped his head down, resting his forehead against hers. "Amanda… what happened earlier…not just with Greg and Chaos, between us…"

Amanda stiffened, then jerked away. "Thank your parents for me. And thank you for getting Chaos to the vet." She climbed back into the Buick. "I think it's safe to say that we should just stay out of each other's way."

She was hurting. He saw that. Well, so was he. But she wasn't thinking clearly. And he couldn't just let her go. Not now. Maybe not ever. "You think so, huh?"

She nodded her head, her sunglasses slipping a little. Just enough that he could see her fresh tears. She pushed them back up.

"Well, does it matter that I don't agree with you?" He clenched his fists, fighting the urge to pull her out of the car and into his arms. His nostrils flared. No, he was not going to lose her.

"Fuck it!" He reached for her.

AMANDA LOOKED UP, surprised at his outburst. Before she could close the door on him, he was hauling her out of the car by her arms, kicking her car door shut.

She opened her mouth to protest but gasped as he lifted her

into his arms and started striding with a determined pace to the nearest barn.

She struggled, pushing against his chest. "What the hell are you doing?"

"What I should do every time you're a pain in my ass."

He nudged the barn door with his shoulder and dumped her unceremoniously on a nearby stack of broken straw bales. He went back to slide the door closed and latched it.

Amanda pushed herself up to a seated position, struggling as her hands sank into the loose straw.

"Don't even move from there."

A shiver ran up her back. Fear? Maybe a little at the unknown, but it wasn't all fear. No matter how many times they'd butted heads, she still wanted him.

"You really deserve to be thrown over my lap and spanked."

She frowned, shaking her head. "You're not going to do that."

"Don't bet on it."

He dropped to his knees beside her, and she quickly started to scramble away.

He grabbed her hair, and the tug on her scalp made her still immediately.

She couldn't tell if he was mad or frustrated or what.

She licked her dry lips. "What do you want from me?" she whispered.

"Nothing." He scrubbed a palm over his short hair. "Everything. *Jesus.*" He reached for her.

"If you're going to do it, just DO IT and get it over with!"

That made him pause. He blew out a breath. "You got it."

He tugged her over his lap by the waist of her jeans. "Pull your pants down."

What? No! He was crazy!

But...

She reached underneath herself and unsnapped her jeans, then worked the zipper down.

Max grabbed both sides and shoved her pants halfway down her thighs. She could feel the cool air on her buttocks. Her pussy clenched, and she struggled to keep from grinding against him.

"Just do it," she moaned and dropped her head against the straw.

He was rock hard against her hip. His hand spread across her ass. Heat against her cool skin. Goosebumps broke out over her body, tightening her nipples to hard points.

His hand disappeared, and she waited for the sharp sting to come. And she waited. Seconds felt like minutes.

She turned her face a little. He was just staring at her. His face unreadable.

"You want me to spank you, don't you?" Not even a question.

She turned her head away from him. "No."

"Little liar."

"I'm not—"

Whap!

She jerked across his lap, his hard length digging deeper into her hip.

"Ow!" She went to rub away the sting, but his voice stopped her.

"No."

Whap!

Her other butt cheek stung. She rose up on her arms and turned to look. Both cheeks had a red mark on them.

She looked up at Max in disbelief. His eyes were dark, his nostrils flared.

"You spanked me!"

He grabbed her hips and lifted her enough so he could move behind her. He tugged her jeans a little lower, making some space between her thighs.

"You loved it."

"No!"

He wrapped an arm under her hips and pulled her ass against him. With his free hand he undid his jeans enough to get his cock out.

"You loved it. You wanted more."

"No!"

"I can see how wet you are, Amanda. I know you want me inside of you."

No. But she couldn't say it out loud. Because it was a lie. She wanted him inside her. Him spanking her surprised her more than hurt. And it made her so wet.

She felt empty, and she needed him to fill her up.

His fingers stroked her pussy, then over the red marks on her ass. Back to her pussy. He dipped them and smoothed the wetness over her pussy lips. He did it again and again. A rhythm that was slowly driving her mad.

His fingers were replaced with the head of his cock. He stroked her with it, rubbing her wetness over himself, teasing her opening with just the tip.

Every time it was right there, just right there, she tried to push back against him, wanting to sink onto his length, but he'd pull back, just far enough for her not to succeed.

She let out a frustrated scream. "Are you going to fuck me?"

"I am." He leaned over her and nipped at the small of her back. He gripped her hip to hold her still. "Are you ready for me?"

She hissed "yesss" at him.

She felt the head of his cock right there again. At her entrance. Any second now...

He asked, "Are you sure?"

Her answering "Fuck you" morphed into a long "fuuuu-uck" as he seated himself deep within her. Her back arched

138

against the pressure of his length bumping her cervix. He was so deep.

He hadn't moved though. Her muscles squeezed him, feeling how full, how hard he was. The pulse at the base of his cock was strong, beating against her clit.

Why was he not moving?

The longer he stayed still, the greater the need grew for her to start thrusting against him. She wanted to come. She needed to come. She needed to lose her mind in an orgasm to drive out everything else that had happened today.

She just wanted to be in that moment. That second. That millisecond.

She turned her head to look at him. His eyes were closed, his mouth slightly parted, and his fingers white from gripping her hips so hard.

"Max..."

His eyes opened, their gazes met, and he finally gave her what she wanted.

He shoved into her. Pounding her. Over and over. A grunt from her, from him.

There was nothing romantic about it. It was raw and angry. It was what she needed; it was what he gave her.

He didn't let up, stroke after hard stroke. He was punishing her in his own way, letting out his frustrations with her. She was accepting every thrust, meeting them, taking him as deep as he could go. She was punishing herself.

He was relentless. And she started to cry. She let go of everything inside her. She was using him to chase out the ugliness of the day. He was using her to do the same.

She didn't want to think about anything else. Just this moment; his desire, her need.

His breathing was ragged; he was close. That realization made her clamp down harder, squeeze him tight.

And then she broke. She cried out as her toes curled and her pussy throbbed around him. A warm gush between her legs. She thought it was him at first, but he was still going. One thrust, another, then he stiffened and cried out, collapsing onto her back. His arms were shaky as he tried to hold his weight off her, but he failed and they both crumpled into a heap on the straw.

She rubbed away the tears on her face and took a deep breath. She wanted him to hold her. To say everything was going to be okay. That Greg would be okay; Chaos would be okay. Life would be perfect.

She rolled away from him and pulled up her pants, keeping her back to him.

"Amanda..."

She found her sunglasses on the barn floor where they had fallen off, and shoved them back on her face, hiding her eyes.

"Amanda!"

Without a word, she slid open the barn door and quickly strode to the car. She was afraid to look toward the farmhouse or back toward the barn.

Every cell in her body was screaming for a meltdown. But she couldn't. She couldn't do that because of Greg. She didn't want to fall apart in front of Max. He'd want to rush in and take care of her, save her.

And deep down she wanted that; she really did. But she had to stand on her own two feet first.

She jumped in and locked the doors, relieved when the car started at the first turn of the key.

She shoved it in reverse and stabbed the gas pedal, the tires kicking up stones.

When she looked in her rearview mirror, Max was leaning against the open barn door, watching the dust rising up as she sped away.

Chapter Twelve

AMANDA SAT on the cold tile floor next to Chaos's cage. Her fingers gripped the wired cage door as she looked at the black-and-white pile lying still inside. Her heart was breaking. She did this. She did this to Chaos. To Greg. To everyone.

She'd had a long conversation with the vet about whether the dog was out of the woods, what his recovery time would be, and what would need to be done after he got released.

Hearing the word *released* gave Amanda some hope that Chaos would really get better, even if it was a slow process. The vet had tried to warn her that the cost was going to be outrageous, but Amanda had just shaken her head and stopped him. She didn't care. She just wanted Chaos fixed, back to normal. She wanted Greg back to normal. Just a boy and his dog.

As she curled up next to his cage, she talked to him. Sometimes, he would just roll his eyes toward her, listening to her voice. Sometimes the end of his tail would thump up and down.

He still had IVs in his shaved legs, and the vet didn't want him to move around and accidentally pull them out, so they had him on tranquilizers. The border collie was such an active dog, she was surprised they actually worked.

He had a cast on his left front leg from a broken bone, and they'd had to pin his right hip because it had been dislocated, so there was a massive surgical scar with stitches there. The vet said that he might need to be taken in and out of the house with a harness that had a handle until he could get around on his own. Chaos was young; he might recover faster than the vet thought.

Amanda hoped so.

Even though Amanda had never owned a pet in her life, she couldn't imagine the house without this chaotic animal.

She visited the dog whenever Greg was at day care, sitting for hours at his cage until the vet techs got tired of her. Sometimes they would lay another dog next to her, fresh out of surgery, so she could stroke the other animal's head while she sang, hummed, or talked to Chaos. It kept her hands busy, and they said it helped the dog come out of anesthesia.

They were probably lying to her, but she didn't care. She continued to do it anyway.

MAX CAME around the corner into the room where the animals needing monitored were kept. He stopped short and backed up a step to hide behind the corner of the door.

Amanda was curled up on the floor next to Chaos's cage, singing a Beyoncé song to the dog.

It was horrible and she'd never be a professional singer, but his heart melted that she didn't care she couldn't carry a tune. That she just wanted to be there for the injured dog, soothing him.

Damn. She surprised him over and over.

He had stopped in to talk to the vet and to check on Chaos's recovery. The vet said nothing about Amanda being there. He had only intended on peeking in on the dog to see how he looked.

A vet tech came behind him and whispered, "She's here a lot. Though we wish she wouldn't sing. Especially since she stays for hours." The tech chuckled and wandered away.

Yeah, he didn't know if he could listen to that for hours either.

He debated whether to walk in and talk to her—and at least make her stop singing—or just leave before she spotted him.

He missed her. He missed her being in his arms...and he wanted to take her in his arms now and comfort her.

But he also didn't want to intrude. She wanted to be independent. She wanted to take responsibility for her brother and his dog.

He understood the independent part. He was the same way. He had always stood strong by himself. Though he had the loving support of his family.

Amanda was only just learning to stand strong on her own. And she had no family support from what he knew.

He wanted to be that support... if she'd allow it.

But he had to tread carefully. With Amanda. And with his mother's overanxious plans to get him hitched to anyone that was in his life longer than a couple hours.

He realized the singing had blissfully stopped and Amanda's head was leaning against the wire cage front, her eyes closed and her breathing steady.

She had drifted off. Max turned on his heels and left the way he came.

Chapter Thirteen

AMANDA LOOKED DOWN at her sports watch. She had an hour before Greg got home. She'd hardly exercised since moving to Manning Grove. A little yoga here and there, but mostly all she had been doing was sitting around the house like a lump, eating all food that she considered "practice." That was... when she wasn't spending time at the vet's.

As she ran past the local elementary school, she spotted ruddy-faced children playing in the schoolyard, all bundled up in their winter coats. A few of them waved as she jogged past. Amanda faintly lifted a hand.

It was cold enough her breath looked like the smoke coming from a train. She was breathing hard from lack of exercise; just running up a slight incline had her groaning with the effort. She vowed to herself to get back on a regular workout regimen. Yoga three times a week. Running another three. Maybe it would relieve some of the stress of—

A truck rolled up next to her and slowed down to her pace. Amanda turned her head as she heard the hum of a power window opening.

Ugh. Wasn't it just over a week ago they had agreed to avoid each other?

Max called through the cab, "What are you doing?"

"Do I really need to answer that?" She turned back to watch her footing. "Go away. I'm busy." Weird—how he had known where to find her? Or had he? Maybe it was just a coincidence.

"Get in."

Amanda pressed her lips together and dodged a drainage grate. She picked up her pace. At the end of the schoolyard she saw an opening in the fence and a patch of woods.

"C'mon, get in."

Amanda made a sudden dash in front of his truck, making him slam on the brakes. Then she took off at a sprint and found just what she was looking for. A little trail through those woods.

She jogged carefully over the rough dirt path until she came out of the trees onto another street. And there was the truck. Parked along the curb.

Max was leaning against it, arms crossed.

"Are you kidding me?"

"What was that about? I could have hit you," Max complained.

Amanda stopped in front of him and put her hands on her hips. Her attempt at looking angry failed as she was forced to bend forward to catch her breath.

"You just like to challenge me, don't you?"

"You know it," she answered, taking a deep breath. She paced in a circle to cool down and prevent a cramp. "I live to challenge you."

He tilted his head toward the vehicle. "C'mon, get in the truck. I want to take you somewhere."

Amanda glanced at her watch again. "Greg's going to be home soon, and I'm not done jogging."

"I'll help you with some cardio later."

Amanda rolled her eyes.

"And Greg is fine; my parents are going to pick him up for the evening."

She stopped her pacing. "What?"

He had made arrangements for her brother without asking her first? So it wasn't coincidence. He had known she was jogging. She wondered if he had a hotline to Mrs. Busybody.

"They were dying to have him over again. They really enjoy spending time with him. And I wanted some time alone with you."

"Oh, what about what I want?"

"I'll take care of that too."

This time Amanda rolled her eyes *and* shook her head. He was so full of himself, thinking he was so irresistible. That she would just comply with any of his wishes. *Hell*, demands.

"What's in this for me?"

"You'll see. Come on." He went around to the passenger side and opened the door for her.

She hesitated before moving around to the side of the truck. "You're like a stalker."

"I am not."

"Right." She climbed in. She hoped she wasn't making a mistake. "Just don't lock the doors in case I have to jump. I don't care if you *are* a cop. Sometimes they are the wackiest. And I thought we sort of agreed to avoid each other."

Max laughed and slammed the passenger door shut. "I didn't agree to that. But we did avoid each other. It's been a few days."

A few days. A few days were like a blink of an eye. Well, maybe not around here it wasn't.

Within minutes, Max pulled the truck into the driveway of a modern cedar A-frame on the outskirts of town. Amanda sucked in a breath as they got closer. The only word that could come to mind was...breathtaking. The sun hit the reddish-gold color of the logs, illuminating the home nestled in a forest of pines. It reminded her of a resort in one of those travel magazines, but on a much smaller scale.

"Whose is this?"

"You'll see."

He parked the truck and helped her out. The house was surrounded by huge old pine trees, some still covered from the last snow, and was completely encircled by a deck. Large windows ran up both sides of a stone chimney.

Max dug deep into his jeans to pull out a set of keys.

"This is yours."

Even though it was more of a statement than a question, he still answered her. "Yep." After unlocking it, he pushed the front door open. "Marc lives with me for now. But if he doesn't start cleaning up after himself, he's going to find himself outside looking in."

"It's beautiful," she said as she went in and looked around. "But what are we doing here? Or should I say, what am I doing here?"

"I'm going to make you dinner."

"Sounds... yummy, I guess." She plucked at her T-shirt. "But I'm sweaty and smelly."

"You can use my shower."

He grabbed her hand and guided her through the house to the master bedroom, not even giving her a chance to snoop around before gently pushing her into the unmistakably masculine en suite bathroom.

"There are towels in the closet. I don't use shampoo—I don't have enough hair to—so you'll just have to make do without. I'll grab you something clean to wear." He turned to go, leaving Amanda standing in the center of the bathroom.

"She didn't leave a bottle?"

He paused, a puzzled look on his face. "Who?"

"Your old girlfriend."

"I've never invited— Never mind, just take a shower."

Amanda shut the door. Once out of sight, she smiled to herself. So far, there were no signs of former feminine presence. She considered that a *good* sign. Or maybe it wasn't. Maybe it was a sign that no female in their right mind wanted to deal with his controlling ass.

She stripped off her soggy jogging clothes, leaving them in a pile on the floor. She started the shower, waiting until the water was good and hot before stepping in.

The hard, humid spray felt good, soothing her tired muscles. She sighed as she turned and turned once more, letting the water calm her nerves from being in Max's shower. In Max's bathroom. In Max's house.

She really never thought about where he lived or in what style he lived. The only thing she knew was that he didn't live with his parents. She had just assumed he lived in an apartment somewhere. But this was a surprise; she never even imagined anything like this.

She shouldn't be surprised though. She knew Max was a determined, hard-working man. If he wanted something, he went after it until he got it.

Her Spidey sense tingled. *If he wanted something, he went after it until he got it.*

She barely heard the rap on the bathroom door before it opened and Max let himself in. Her heart flipped suddenly, her pulse started pounding when she heard him over the shower.

"Phew, it's steamy in here. Do you need help scrubbing your back?"

His blurred figure was barely visible through the opaque shower door—the only barrier between him and her naked body. "I can manage."

"I can reach all those places you can't."

Amanda stilled under the hot stinging spray. Her teeth tugged at her lower lip.

"'Manda?"

His deep voice just saying her name like a caress made her toes curl in the swirl of the water. The bar of soap slipped from her fingers. It clunked loudly against the shower floor.

"Amanda, are you okay?" Max opened the stall door and stopped mid-motion. "You are definitely okay. *Hell.*"

Thin rivers of water streamed down her body, making her aware of every inch of skin that he could see. She raised her eyes from the fallen soap to look at the man who was staring at her like she was every man's fantasy. He could do that. He could make her feel so wanted... so desired. And at that moment, she only wanted to be one man's fantasy.

She let out a shaky breath.

"Are you coming out or am I coming in?" His grin was crooked and strained as if he was struggling to control himself.

"Both." She reached out to take a handful of his T-shirt and pulled him into the shower. The water quickly soaked his clothes. She wrapped her arms around his neck and stood on tiptoes, leaning her bare body against him. "Kiss me."

He bent his head and murmured against her lips, "I'm so glad these boots are waterproof," and captured her lips with his.

He explored the deep recesses of her mouth while brushing his thumbs over her taut nipples, driving her completely out of her mind. The kiss broke as she gasped. He raised his head slightly. "You know, I'd love to fuck you in the shower, but it would take me a while to peel out of these wet jeans. So I have another idea."

Max backed her up against the tile wall and dropped to his knees.

It wasn't to pick up the soap.

He placed her hands on his shoulders and lifted her leg up until it also was balanced on his broad shoulder.

He had one hand against her belly, supporting her as he kissed the outer edge of her pussy lips, his tongue dipping inside, tasting her.

His other hand spread her apart, and he sucked at her clit until fire started deep within her belly. Her breasts felt large and heavy, her nipples hard. She sucked in her stomach and tilted her pelvis, giving him better access. The warm water from the shower with the combination of his tongue made a groan escape her. She let her head drop back against the tile, and she closed her eyes. She didn't want to see his dark head between her thighs; she wanted to feel him. She wanted to focus solely on the sensations he was causing with his fingers and his tongue. He stroked her, nipped her, sucked her. Fingers plucked at her clit, slid into to her and curved.

He touched that spot and stroked it. Again and again. It made both her jaw and pussy clench against the bizarre but deeply arousing sensation. He strummed her like a guitar, tuning her up. She bit her bottom lip and cried out. Her back arched uncontrollably. He wouldn't stop. His lips on her clit, his fingers searching, stroking. She wanted to scream at him to stop, that it was unbearable. She couldn't take any more.

The orgasm started at her toes, curling them, as the shock waves ran up her legs, into her pussy, exploding. She cried out again. Her fingers dug into his shoulders as she tried to avoid collapsing. But he drew away and stood, giving her a brush of his lips before taking her into his arms.

She tensed for a second, then relaxed into him and whispered, "Was it as good for you as it was for me?"

Her body vibrated with his deep chuckle.

As Max puttered around his kitchen making dinner, Amanda took the time to explore his home. Dressed in one of his old T-shirts and an even older pair of boxer shorts, she made short work of inspecting every room.

The house was beautiful. Amanda guessed it to be about five years old. The furniture was minimal and rustic, fitting in nicely with the hewed-log walls. A few pictures of his family were sprinkled around the living room, but curiously, not one of them included a woman besides his mother. His bed—which looked handmade—was huge and inviting; she thought about how they could make use of it later.

She also discovered Marc's room—it was one of only three rooms on the second floor—and agreed with Max. Greg was actually neater, and from what she saw, Marc wasn't hard to beat. She shut the door quickly before anything crawled out.

The showpiece of the house was the immense fireplace spanning from floor to ceiling in the two-story living room. Built from mountain stone, it was flanked by the large windows she had seen from outside. Amanda imagined herself lounging in front of a roaring fire on a frosty winter night, gazing through those tall windows at the fresh-fallen snow clinging to the huge old pine trees.

What was she thinking? Snow? She hated the cold.

Miami. Heat. White beaches. Warm water. Sexy bodies in skimpy bathing suits. Color. Culture.

That's what she should be thinking about. Not snow. Did she really want to spend another winter here in this desolate town? A clatter from the kitchen broke into her thoughts.

This was never going to work. Max was a man from Manning Grove. Small-town cop. She was a woman from Miami. Big city... what? Big-city party girl? She didn't have an answer. She just didn't know anymore.

In Miami, she'd had no direction. She had just lived for the moment.

Now, she had the responsibility of her brother. She finally had a purpose. Maybe a path she had not or would not have chosen for herself, but a direction nonetheless.

A louder bang came from the kitchen, then a muffled curse.

Leaving her thoughts behind, Amanda moved toward the kitchen area. "Need help?"

Max was leaning over the sink, intently shaking something. "No. Go away. I'll call you when I'm ready."

"Where do you want me to go? This house is like one big open room. And I'm definitely not going upstairs again; that should be marked off as hazardous."

"Why don't you take a walk outside around the deck? It goes all the way around the house. Dinner won't be long now."

"Okay. It better be worth the wait." She grabbed his jacket by the front door and slipped into it. The sleeves were so long on her that she couldn't even see her hands. Pulling the jacket tighter around her, she opened the nearby French doors and stepped outside to give him some peace. She plunked down in an Adirondack chair to wait.

Five minutes later, Max popped his head out the door. "It's ready."

Her stomach growled noisily in response.

The crinkles around his eyes were evident in the late afternoon sun. Amanda realized that those creases really stood out when he was pleased. Not to mention relaxed.

He stepped close and offered her a hand out of the chair. As she stood, he pulled her into his arms. He framed her face with his hands and placed a soft kiss across her nose. "We could skip dinner."

"You worked too hard. Let's go eat. I'm hungry." Her empty belly complained again.

"Me too. Just not for food." He took her hand, led her back into the house, and then helped her out of his jacket. She was surprised when she saw the rough-cut table. It was set beautifully with stoneware dinner plates; glowing candles illuminated the settings. A pair of oversize glasses of red wine twinkled in the candlelight.

Amanda was touched with the effort he'd taken. She was sure this was a rare occurrence—Max making a romantic dinner. He even pulled out a chair for her.

Amanda threw her napkin across her lap, then wondered why, since she was wearing old boxer shorts. She tossed it next to her plate instead. "What are we having?"

"Squirrel stew."

"What?"

"Just kidding. I made a couple of venison steaks, baby red potatoes, and a salad."

Amanda frowned. "What's venison?"

Without meeting her glance, he said, "It's like beef."

He uncovered the dishes and served her, then himself. He lifted his glass of wine. "Let's make a toast."

Amanda followed suit by raising hers.

"To—"

Amanda started as the front door crashed open. Marc bounded in, dropping his patrol bag by the front door with a *thump*.

"Hey, Max! Why are all the lights off— *Oh*." Marc stopped in his tracks. With a smirk, he took in the scene in front of him. "Sorry, I didn't know that..." He shrugged helplessly. "Oops."

Max put his untouched wineglass down with exaggerated care.

Amanda watched various emotions cross his face before he spoke. His words were drawn out very slowly. "I thought you were on second shift today."

"I was. The chief sent me home early. Dunn wanted some OT." Marc stepped up to the table and looked down at their plates. "Are those the steaks from my buck?"

"Buck?" Amanda didn't think she'd heard right.

"Yes," Max answered his brother.

"What's a buck?" She shot a probing look toward Max, who abruptly found his wineglass very mesmerizing.

The explanation came from Marc instead. "A male deer."

"Do you mean you were going to have me eat a deer? Like Bambi?" She looked at both men in disbelief. "Marc, did you shoot Bambi?"

"No, I shot Bambi's dad."

"Oh please, let's not get into a debate about hunting. Now's not the time." Max stood up and grabbed his brother by the arm, steering him away from the table. He said through clenched teeth, "Get lost."

Marc laughed before saying loudly, "I guess I'll go take the ATV out for a ride."

"Make it a long one."

"How long?" Marc nudged his older brother. "You shouldn't take too long—"

Max growled, "Marc."

"Okay, okay. I'm out of here." Marc gave Amanda a parting glance. "By the way, nice outfit. Your boxer shorts are gaping."

With a sharp intake of breath, Amanda shifted the enormous tee over her lap. Max shoved Marc toward the door.

"All right! I'm going. Jeez."

Max held out his hand.

Marc eyed it cautiously, facing his older brother from the entranceway. "What?"

"Your house key."

"What!"

Max refrained from saying anything and just jiggled his hand.

"Hell." Marc dug in his pocket, pulled a key off his key ring, and dropped it into Max's palm. "How am I going to get back in?"

"I'll unlock the door when it's... safe."

"So, what am I supposed to do—"

Max slammed the door shut and twisted the lock. He returned to the table and settled back into his chair. He gave Amanda a rueful smile. "Sorry. We won't be disturbed again. At least for a while."

"You didn't have to kick him out. He lives here too."

"Only due to my generosity, which I'm not feeling right now. So, let's eat."

"I don't know," she said, eyeing the now lukewarm steak on her plate as if it was road kill. She had no problem eating meat. She loved meat. She could never be a vegetarian or a vegan, even though most of her friends back in Miami were. Not her, she loved a big, juicy burger. But deer? That poor four-legged, adorably sweet, big-eyed...

"Amanda, just try it. I promise you'll love it." He lifted his wineglass back up. "But first, let's finish that toast."

Amanda lifted her glass in response.

"To a truce."

Yes, Amanda could agree with that. "Okay." The glasses rang as they tapped their rims together.

He nodded at her to try the meal.

Amanda picked up her steak knife and tentatively dug in. Placing a small piece on her tongue, she chewed carefully, critically. Surprised how lean but tender the steak was, she had to admit that it was delicious. And she was starving.

Max watched her warily as she ate, but visibly relaxed when Amanda finished off the meal in record time. "Well?"

"It was okay."

"Liar."

"Okay, it was great. But I still don't know if I'm comfortable knowing what I ate."

"If you liked that, wait until you try deer bologna."

"I'll wait."

Max chuckled. The low rumble sent a shot of warmth through her. Every time he laughed or smiled or just grinned, it surprised her. Normally he seemed so serious about everything. It was refreshing to see him lighten up.

He took a sip of wine before asking, "So, how's Chaos?"

She gave him a crooked smile. "I know you've been there to check on him. One of the vet techs told me you've stopped by a few times."

"Have you taken Greg?"

Amanda shook her head. "I don't want to upset him. I give him updates, and he's looking forward to Chaos coming home."

"I'm sure," he murmured. "Do you have an idea when?"

She ran her finger around the rim of her wineglass. "No, I wish I did. Greg asks multiple times a day. He's like a broken record."

"Do you want me to pick him up when he's released?"

Amanda regarded the man across from her. "Why would you want to do that?"

He reached across the table to cover her hand with his. "I just want to help."

His thumb brushing back and forth over her knuckles distracted her. "I can handle it. I'll pick him up when Greg's at day care so Chaos is settled in before my brother gets home."

"Well... if you need help..."

Max wanted her to need him. She could see it in his face. "Thanks. But we'll be fine."

It was nice of him to offer, but again, he was putting himself into the mix when this was something she could handle on her own. She needed to prove to herself that she could handle these responsibilities. Even though the accident a few days ago made it clear she still had a ways to go. But if she let Max constantly help her, she'd never move forward. She didn't want to rely on anyone anymore.

Not even the cop across from her.

As she got to know him better, she really couldn't imagine him in any other field. But then the apple usually didn't fall far from the tree, and he was definitely following in his father's footsteps. As were his brothers. Except for the settling-down part, that is.

"Did you become a cop right after the Marines?"

"Yeah. I enlisted while I was in my senior year. I helped my parents on the farm the summer right out of high school, then went to Parris Island for boot camp." He grimaced. "It was the hardest thirteen weeks of my life." His gaze got distant as if he was remembering what he'd had to go through.

"Did you ever want to quit?"

"Never." He squeezed her fingers.

She couldn't imagine this man would quit anything in his life.

"I didn't go there to just quit. My father was a Marine. And I damn well was going to be one too. Plus, I knew that was my brothers' path as well. I had to set an example."

He seemed the type of guy who wanted to lead by example. He'd probably make a good police chief one day.

"Were you deployed?"

He blinked. Maybe he was surprised that she was even interested. Or maybe he didn't want to talk about it. "Yeah. I did a couple tours in Iraq."

"Was it scary?"

"It certainly wasn't a vacation. I did my four years and I was out. Unfortunately, my brother keeps going back. His leave at

Christmas was way too short. He's done his time, and I'm not sure why he doesn't get out while he's still alive."

"The way your mom talks, she worries about him a lot." When he gave her a curious look, she realized she'd almost blown it. "I mean she seemed to worry about him a lot when he was home at Christmas."

"We all do. Being in the Middle East has changed him. I guess it changed Marc and me too, but not like it has changed Matt. He has a good job waiting for him. Not sure why he's not taking advantage of it." Max cleared his throat and got back on track. "So, when I got out of the Marines, I took a couple weeks off until the next municipal police academy class started in Harrisburg."

"How long was that?"

He looked at her curiously. "This isn't boring you?"

She shook her head.

"Twenty-four weeks. It was cake compared to Parris Island. I couldn't believe the whining I heard from some of the cadets."

"Is it something I could get through?"

Max released her hand and sat back. Mixed emotions crossed his face before he said, "The academy? Sure. You'd get through it. Do you want to become a police officer?"

"Oh, hell no. I'm just messing with you." But she couldn't miss the rush of air from his lungs as he relaxed.

Did he really feel like she could make it through the academy, or was he just being possessive and overprotective by not wanting her to become a cop?

Max pushed his chair back and stood. "C'mon. Help me clean up."

Amanda rose and followed him into the spacious kitchen, carrying a load of dirty dishes. As she started rinsing them, Max went back and brought them their wineglasses. After topping them off first, of course.

She reached out a sudsy hand to accept hers and took a long sip. Then she returned her attention to her task, handing the rinsed dishes to Max to load into the dishwasher. When they were done, she washed her hands. She turned in place and Max was immediately there, handing her a towel.

"Thanks for dinner... and for earlier." She gave him a tentative smile and took another long sip of her wine.

Max reached out, taking her glass from her. "Let's get our thanks out of the way." He lifted one of her hands and kissed the palm. "Thank you."

"For what?"

"You'll see." He reached out, curving his hand behind her neck under her long wavy hair, pulling her closer. He leaned down so he could stroke her lips with the tip of his tongue, tasting the tart, fruity residue. "I think that the wine tastes better on you."

"Let me try it," she said, huskily. She studied his every move as he raised his glass to take a sip, leaving a trail of wine glistening over his lips. She stood on tiptoe, stretching her body against him, feeling his every male angle. Amanda covered his mouth with hers, licking and stroking. She pulled back slightly, their breath mingling. "Mmm. You're right."

He refilled their glasses once again before leading her across the living room into the master bedroom. The only light was the sun setting through the windows, giving the room a rosy hue.

He drew her to the bed, urging her to lie down. Max knelt on the mattress to slowly slip off the old T-shirt and the boxer shorts she was wearing, making sure his fingers, knuckles, and arms brushed her here...and there. When Amanda was naked, he sat back on his heels to study her.

Amanda brought up her arms, an ineffective shield. "Don't."

One eyebrow rose. "Why?"

"You're still dressed. That's unfair."

"I can remedy that." Max climbed off the bed and took his time baring his body for her, making sure she didn't miss a thing. Not one hardened plane, rough angle, or smooth surface. When he was done, he stood proudly, fully aroused, a fact Amanda found hard to ignore. She bit her lip. He was finely chiseled and very, very hard to resist.

But she already knew that.

Max grabbed his wineglass from the nightstand and said, "Lay back. I want to enjoy some more wine."

He tilted the glass over her navel and filled it to the brim. He caught the overflow with his lips, stroking the tender skin of her belly with his tongue. He then dipped a finger in her navel and drew the warm liquid over her body like finger paint. Every line Max created, he erased it with his tongue.

Amanda felt pinned in place, not wanting to move, as she watched him with narrowed eyes. She could barely stand the torture. But she resisted reaching for him, fought off demanding he fill her up. She wanted the torment to last a little longer. Just a little more...just to the edge.

Max was having a difficult time holding back, as was evident by his nostrils flaring as he fought for air. Amanda felt him trembling slightly as he attempted to restrain himself. His fingers explored her warm, wet spots while his tongue painted pictures over her heated skin. He nuzzled her breast with his cheek and turned his face just enough to pull her nipple into his mouth. He tugged gently with his teeth until she cried out.

Her panting and whimpers made him move quicker, more urgently until he couldn't wait any longer. Until she couldn't wait any longer.

He rose over her and drove himself home.

He gave her what she had wanted in the shower earlier. Not that she was complaining. He was skilled with his tongue, lips, and fingers. But there was nothing like the pressure of his body against her as he filled her emptiness with long strokes. She tilted her hips to take him deeper, matching his movements thrust after thrust.

She grabbed his ass, the tight muscles flexing under her fingers with every pump. Every brush of his pelvis against her clit made her cry out, made her pussy bloom with wanting more, wanting him deeper, if that was even possible.

She bucked harder against him.

"You're so open. I can feel you pulsating around my cock," he rasped. "You're driving me mad."

Me as well, she thought. She couldn't get enough of him.

Normally, they were oil and water; tonight they were fluid together. Meshed.

He gently nipped the fleshy part of her breast, then soothed it with his tongue. Worked his magic over both breasts, nipping and licking, avoiding the hard nubs of her nipples. She wanted his mouth on them; she whimpered and wiggled against him, trying to get his mouth closer.

He propped himself up on his arms and looked at her. Really looked at her. She couldn't pull her gaze away. His eyes were dark, unreadable. A shudder ran through her.

She couldn't want this man any more than at this moment.

He finally relented and sucked a nipple into his mouth, teasing it with his tongue, plucking at it with his lips.

A jolt shot through her core, deep through her belly, and into her pussy.

She gasped as she felt the waves start. "I'm going to come."

He grunted and picked up the pace even more. He gyrated against her, grinding into her swollen clit.

She went over the edge, releasing a low wail. His head dropped next to hers, his lips next to her ear, and he groaned, "Fuck."

One last thrust and he stilled deep inside her, the base of his cock pulsating against her as he released.

"Damn," both said simultaneously, then laughed at their similar response.

Damn was right.

He slid to her side and gathered her in his arms.

With the glow of the lowering sun and the afterglow of great sex, Amanda let out a long, contented sigh and stretched like a cat from fingertip to toe. She was full—from dinner and from Max. Her appetizer and her dessert.

Tonight was so different from the barn. They were like two different people. No anger. No frustration. They were relaxed and not arguing. It was weird. They *were* like oil and water, and Amanda was waiting for the other hunting boot to drop.

MAX OPENED the bathroom door to see Amanda practically hidden in his bed. He fought the urge to climb back in bed with her and bury himself deep in her once again. He wanted to make her mew and whimper as he had done earlier. But—

He shook his head, clearing his thoughts.

He carried her now dry running clothes in his arms. He dumped them at the foot of the bed. "Your clothes are dry enough to put on now."

Amanda ignored him, snuggling deeper with a sigh.

"Amanda."

A muffled "what?" came from beneath the sheets.

"What do you mean, what? It's getting late."

Amanda pulled the sheet back and shifted herself up. She looked at the digital clock on the nightstand. "It's only eight o'clock. Why don't you just call your parents? I'm sure they won't mind if Greg stayed overnight."

"No." There was no way he was calling his mother and telling her to keep Greg overnight. That was the last thing he needed. It was bad enough that Marc now had more fodder to torment him. That was unavoidable. But he did not need his mother knowing his *personal* business. And she certainly didn't need to know that they were sleeping together. Which was what she'd assume if he asked them to keep Greg overnight.

Then she'd be asking questions. And pestering. About settling down. About marriage. About children. Max let out a mental groan. No, thanks.

"What do you mean no? No, you don't want to burden your parents, or no, you don't want me staying here overnight."

Max realized that this might be a touchy subject. But there was no way to steer clear of it. No matter what he said, it was going to be misconstrued. Maybe he could just say nothing. "We talked about this before."

"So?"

"So? So my mother, that's the so."

As good as Amanda looked in his bed... It looked too right, too comfortable. Like she belonged there. His chest tightened. Max wasn't ready for that. He wasn't ready for permanent. He wasn't prepared for someone so young...no, not young, *youthful*. Youthful? Immature, naive, maybe. He scrubbed a hand over his short hair.

It might have been a mistake to bring her into his domain. To let her in. To let her in his home—his privacy, his personal space. Pain shot through his temple.

"I think you need to get dressed and we need to go pick up Greg."

She rolled out of bed, snagged her clothes, and got dressed quickly. She flung open his bedroom door and took long strides out of the room.

"Seriously, you don't want her picking out china patterns,"

Max called after her, close on her heels. He came up short when he saw Marc standing in front of Amanda, his finger over his lips and a spare key swinging from his finger. Max forgot about the spare key. *Damn.*

"Marc, can you take me home?"

Marc's mouth opened, but nothing came out. He looked like a deer caught in headlights. Quite possibly like the deer they had eaten earlier.

"No," Max answered for him as he came up behind her. "I'll take you home."

"No. I don't want to *inconvenience* you. Marc, will you take me home?"

Max gave his brother a dirty look, hoping that Marc would be smart enough not to get involved in the conflict between him and Amanda.

"Uh..."

"No. I will do it," Max insisted, an edge to his voice.

Amanda glared at Max. "No, you won't." She turned toward Marc and gave him a pleading look. "Please?"

Marc glanced over her head to his brother. Max gave his head a slight shake.

"Uh, I don't think it's a good idea."

That was his brother! He was getting the hint.

"I don't care what you guys think is a good idea. Marc, you are taking me home. If you don't, I'm going to walk."

There was no way she was walking home. "You can't—"

Marc pitched in. "It's too far—"

"Amanda, it's getting dark—"

"Watch me." With a determined step she strode out the front door.

"Okay, okay! I'll drive you home," Marc called as he quickly followed behind her.

Max threw up his hands and sighed as he watched his

brother hurry after Amanda. He stood in the doorway helplessly as they both got into Marc's truck and left.

"Damn," he whispered. His stubbornness had screwed things up royally. Once again.

He slammed the front door shut and leaned back against it, cursing himself.

Pushing himself off the door, Max began to pace back and forth. He had to make things right. He was mad that he couldn't express himself the way he wanted to when he was with her. He didn't know how to deal with it. He didn't know if he *could* deal with it. But he didn't want her to walk out of his life, either way.

He had to call her.

She had been out running earlier, so he knew she didn't have her cell phone, plus Max wouldn't want to have the conversation with her while she was still with Marc anyway. That would be inviting never-ending mocking from his brothers, both family and on the force.

So, he dialed her house phone; he would just leave a message for now. As expected, the machine answered, but he hung up quickly. He had to think about what to say. He had to get it right the first time.

He dialed again. This time he let the machine get to the beep.

"'Manda. I'm sorry. I..." He hit the End button with a curse.

He dialed again. *Beep.* "Amanda, I know you're angry." *Of course, she's angry, you stupid ass.* He cut the call off.

Beep. "Mandy, can you call me back? I need to talk to you." He hung up again.

Fuck. He was such an ass.

"WE'VE GOT to stop at your parents' house to pick up Greg," Amanda said as they headed back toward town.

The surprised look that Marc gave her was his only answer.

They drove in uncomfortable silence to his parents. Amanda sat fuming in the truck while Marc ran in and got Greg. Amanda shifted over to the center of the bench seat to let her brother in.

Amanda couldn't decide if she was more angry or hurt at Max's remarks.

Marc made compulsory conversation with Greg on their way back to the Barber house. Once there, Greg slid out and ran to the porch, while Marc grabbed Amanda's arm.

"Hold on." He cleared his throat. "I don't know what happened back there, but I know you are boiling mad."

"That's putting it mildly."

"Yeah, well, I know my brother. He can be dumb sometimes. Hell, we all can. But I think he... *feels* something for you. I've never seen him act this way before. Never. I mean I've seen him date women and... well, you know. But he has never brought anyone back to his house. He has never invited anyone over to our parents' before. I think he's feeling scared... no, not scared... trapped? No!" Marc smacked the heel of his hand into his forehead. "I didn't mean it like that. Can you get the drift on what I am trying to say?"

"And?"

"Well, I just wanted you to know."

"So now I know. Thank you for the ride."

Before she could shut the door, he said one more thing. "Oh, and by the way, he's right. You don't want Ma getting wind of anything because she *will* be picking out china patterns. If you think Max is stubborn, you don't know my mother."

Amanda watched Marc drive away before she let Greg into the house with the spare key she had hidden under the mat when she had gone running. She was sure Max wouldn't like that idea. The officer in him would think it unsafe. Predictable. The spot an intruder would first look.

Who cared what Max would think?

"Can I's have a snack?" Greg asked her eagerly.

"Sure."

She followed her brother into the kitchen and poured him a glass of milk. She made him sit at the table, then dug out a container of her homemade brownies. She snapped off the lid and plopped the container in front of Greg, who within a matter of seconds sported a milk mustache.

When she turned away, she noticed the answering machine blinking. The number four flashed at her like a beacon. Who would leave four messages? Neither Carlos nor her mother had the house number. She tapped the Caller ID button on the machine as it scrolled through the last four callers.

Bryson, M.

Bryson, M.

Bryson, M.

Bryson, M.

Amanda located the button she was looking for.

Delete.

Delete.

Delete.

Delete.

She turned back to Greg and sank into the chair across from him. "Can I have a brownie?" Or two?

Chapter Fourteen

Mary Ann glanced over at Amanda, who was doing her best to ignore the insistent ringing of her cell phone in the background. When her cell phone wasn't ringing, the house phone was.

"Sweetie, you aren't going to answer that?"

"No, it'll go to voicemail." From the living room, the *beep* of the machine sounded. "Or the answering machine. See?"

With a slight shrug of her shoulders, Mary Ann pulled the cookbook closer. She laid a finger on the page. "This tells you to sift the flour first. Since you don't have a sifter, this is what you do. Give me a cup of that flour."

Amanda popped the lid off the Tupperware container and dipped the plastic measuring cup into the flour, creating a puff of white dust. She choked as she involuntarily inhaled some, the force of her cough causing an even greater cloud. She wrinkled her nose, trying not to sneeze.

She gladly handed the cup over to Mary Ann, who shook her head. Amusement twitched the older woman's lips as she dumped the flour into a strainer. "Now I'll just hold it over the bowl and tap it gently. You don't want a cloud. That will sift the flour well enough—"

Her cell phone rang again.

Mary Ann dropped the makeshift sifter to plant her hands on her hips. "Amanda, how do you know that it's not important? Someone must really want to talk to you."

She was right. Amanda couldn't put it off any longer. She was going to have to deal with *the caller* at some point. It might as well be now. She snatched up her cell from the kitchen table. "I'll take it in the living room."

Amanda braced herself as she went into the other room and answered. She didn't need the caller ID to know who it was. "What?" Right now he didn't even deserve the courtesy of a "hello."

For a moment there was silence.

"Hey. Uh, I was surprised you answered."

"Well, I figured I'd better before you killed my cell phone's battery."

"Yeah, well, I'm sure you know I've been trying to reach you by all the messages I've left."

"Oh? I haven't heard any of the messages."

"'Manda, I know you're upset, but—"

"But nothing."

"Just hear me out."

"I heard you, Max, and I didn't like how you said it."

She heard a long sigh through the phone; then Max replied, "I can't do this on the phone."

"Me, neither, so stop calling."

"I'm coming over." He was clearly determined.

Amanda thought of his mother in the other room. "Now is not a good time." Wouldn't he be shocked to find out how much time they'd been spending together?

"It's as good a time as any. I'll be over in ten minutes." He hung up before she could get in another word.

She ended the call and looked toward the kitchen. Let him show up; he was only going to embarrass himself in front of his own mother.

He didn't want his mother finding out what was going on between them the other night. Well, he wouldn't be able to avoid it now.

She went back to the kitchen to finish her red velvet cake lesson.

———

NINE MINUTES and twenty-two seconds later, Max rang the doorbell.

He was nervous; he rubbed his damp palms against his jeans.

He sucked in a breath when Amanda opened the door. She was wearing a pink tank top and skintight black yoga pants. Her long hair was pulled back into a ponytail. Without a stitch of makeup on, she reminded him of a high school cheerleader. A very perky one at that.

He reached out his index finger to brush white powder off the tip of her nose.

"Are you staying out of trouble?" He rubbed his fingers together and brought it up to his nose to sniff. "What is this?"

Amanda rolled her eyes. "Puh-leez. It's flour."

"I knew that."

"Right." When Amanda turned away, he followed her inside. "So, what do you want, Max?"

"I don't like the way we left it the other night."

Once in the living room, she walked over to the antique secretary's desk and found sudden interest in it. She let out a long, deep sigh. "Neither do I."

"So, what are we going to do about it?"

"Look, you're the one who had to come over here. What are *you* going to do about it?"

He swung her around to face him, studying her. An instant later he released her and stepped back. "Apologize. Say that I'm sorry for being such an idiot. Tell you I wanted you to stay; I really did. But..."

"But?"

"But... you heard my mother at Christmas. All she does is nag the three of us to get married and produce children. I just don't want to give her... false hope."

"So, basically what you're saying is that you're not looking for anything permanent." She straightened, standing a little taller. "Well, maybe neither am I. I don't know how long I'll be here in Manning Grove. As soon as I can convince Greg that he'd be happier in Miami, we're leaving."

That wasn't what he wanted to hear. She was just blowing smoke. Because there was no way he was going to let her leave. Ever. This was her home now. This was Greg's home. She had to stay. He liked spending time with her—when they weren't rubbing each other the wrong way. He liked when they were rubbing each other the *right* way.

"No." He shook his head. "No, I like you, Amanda. I really do. I thought it was obvious. But whatever is going to happen between us... whatever is happening between us, I want to do on my own timeline. Not my mother's. Can you understand that?"

"Oh yeah. I can understand not wanting someone else to make decisions for you."

"I deserve that. I get it." He shifted closer to capture her hips, pulling her just a breath away. "But I do know one thing..." He brushed his lips along her temple, winding his fingers in her ponytail, and tugged gently until her head tilted back, exposing her neck. He nuzzled the little dip at the base of her neck, then moved to capture her lips. She tasted so good—

"Sweetie, we need to finish making the cream-cheese icing for —" Mary Ann stopped. "Oh! Oh, Max! Hi, honey. I thought I heard voices out here."

"Mom!" He dropped his arms, quickly stepping away from Amanda. Heat crawled up his neck. He cleared his throat. "What are you doing here?"

"Why, I come over here all the time. Amanda didn't tell you?"

He closed his gaping mouth with a snap. He shot a look at Amanda before replying, "No."

"I'm teaching her to cook. We are having so much fun together. She's going to make someone a great wife."

Max groaned. This was what he was trying to avoid: his mother seeing Amanda as daughter-in-law material. And even worse, his mother thought she was training her to be a good wife. This wasn't good. This was extremely bad.

"How did you get here? I didn't see your vehicle out front."

"Your father dropped me off."

His father knew what his mother was doing and hadn't warned him? Max was going to have a talk with him.

Max approached his mother, taking her elbow firmly. "I'll take you home."

His mother jerked her arm away. "No, Amanda and I have to finish this red velvet cake."

"You can finish it another time."

His mother looked at him with disbelief. "No, Max. Your father will pick me up. But I'll go back into the kitchen and give you two a couple minutes alone." She winked knowingly at him.

Max gritted his teeth. His mother went back into the kitchen with the mistaken belief that they needed some privacy.

Max whispered fiercely, "What are you doing?"

"Baking."

"How long has this been going on? How much does she know?" His voice lifted and then cracked like a teenage boy's.

Fuck!

"About us?" Amanda shrugged. "She's not stupid, Max."

They stood staring at each other in a standoff: ice blue versus emerald green. The seconds ticked by in silence.

"Sweetie, are you coming?" Mary Ann called from the next room.

Keeping a steady, pointed gaze, a wicked smile crossed Amanda's face. "Yes, Ma. I'll be right there."

Max was the first to break eye contact as he grabbed his chest. "Ma?" What was that shooting pain in his chest? He was having a heart attack. "Why are you calling my mother Ma?"

"She said I could. It's her initials. Mary Ann... Ma, get it?"

The hole in the earth was widening; he might as well just leap in now. His mother was hanging out with the woman he'd been sleeping with. The woman he'd been sleeping with was calling his mother "Ma."

"That's screwed up. I've—I've got to sit down." He sank onto the nearby couch, pinching the bridge of his nose.

"No, it isn't. It's great. She's a great mother, and you should be proud of her."

"Oh, I am." Proud that she'd found someone to groom to be his future wife. Proud that she has stuck her nose where it didn't belong. Hey, that sounded familiar. How many times had Amanda accused him of doing the same? Like mother, like son? He grimaced.

"She has been spending her spare time teaching me to cook and bake because I *asked*." Amanda shook her head. "All I had to do was ask her. And you know what? She was thrilled that I asked."

"You could have asked me."

"To teach me to cook?"

"No, damn it. You should have asked me first if I minded my mother—" Max stopped, watching Amanda's face darken. *Oh shit.*

He stood up quickly and caught her arms before he got belted in the mouth. With a sigh, he let her arms go. If she cracked him upside the head, he deserved it.

He had come over to apologize for being a jerk, and here he was again... being a fucking jerk. It was becoming a pattern for him. One he needed to break.

"Amanda, I came over here to apologize for the other night. I did it, and now I am apologizing for what I just said. And let me just get this out of the way now: I'm sorry for every asinine thing I do or say in the future. There, that should just about cover it."

"If you think a simple apology is going to be a Band-Aid for all our—*your* problems... Well, it's not. Your apologies come too little, too late. If you think you can do or say what you want, that you can be bossy, try to control my life, and then just say, 'I'm sorry' when you want to get me into bed? And then everything is all right? It doesn't work that way. It hasn't. It won't. It never will."

"You know, we need to talk about this more when *my mother*," his eyebrows rose, "isn't twenty feet away in the next room." He jabbed his finger a few times toward the kitchen.

"Fine."

"Fine what?"

"We can talk about it later."

"Oh." He wasn't expecting her to be so agreeable. That was a switch. Wait a minute. There probably was a catch. Or it was a trap. With caution, he asked, "Okay, when?"

"Tonight. After Greg goes to bed."

"When's that?"

"Come around nine."

Mary Ann peeked her head out of the kitchen. "Max, honey, why don't you come help us finish up this cake?"

Panic shot through him. "Got to go, Mom!" he yelled. To Amanda he whispered, "See you at nine." He took one last look at her "cheerleader" outfit. "Don't change."

Then he bolted; he had to get out the door before he got roped into wearing an apron.

AFTER MAKING sure Greg was tucked into bed, Amanda stayed a few minutes by his bedside, talking with him until, after a final yawn, he drifted off to sleep.

She had just descended the stairs when she heard a soft rap on the front door.

This was one of the few times that she had known beforehand that she was going to see Max, and she had been anxious ever since he had left earlier. In fact, the rest of the velvet cake lesson had pretty much been a waste, as she couldn't pay attention. Mary Ann had given up and had taken the un-iced cake home to finish it herself.

Amanda's pulse raced as she went to let Max in.

When she opened the door, she stood there mesmerized for a moment. He was wearing a worn—so worn that they were almost white—pair of jeans that fit real nicely. And under his leather jacket, she noticed a snug black T-shirt that she was sure would expose that tattoo—the one that drew her eyes every time. As her inspection moved upward past his broad shoulders, she noticed he hadn't shaved the five o'clock shadow he had been sporting earlier—and it was damn sexy. The only thing that stopped him from looking like a full-blown rebel was the severe law-enforcement haircut. Not enough hair there to run her fingers through or to grip onto when—

"Done?" He raised one eyebrow and grinned. "Want me to strip right here on the stoop, or can I come in first?"

Amanda answered him with a smile and stepped back, but not enough to give him room. He had to turn sideways and brush against her to enter the house.

"Oh, you're evil. I'm supposed to be here to talk, Amanda, remember?"

She shut the door and locked it. "I remember. Let's go into the sunroom. That way we won't disturb Greg."

As they walked through the kitchen, she nodded her head toward the screened addition. "Go on in. I'll get us a snack."

Within a minute she had thrown some of her cookies onto a plate and carried them into the sunroom.

Max was sitting relaxed in the love seat, his legs stretched out in front of him, his ankles crossed. He had turned on only one of the table lamps, giving the room a soft radiance. Soft and romantic.

Amanda shook her head to clear it.

He looked at the plate hungrily. "Peanut butter?"

"Yep."

"What happened to that red velvet cake you were making earlier?"

"Your mom took it with her for the ladies at bingo."

She didn't want to tell him that Mary Ann had taken it unfinished, complaining good-naturedly about certain young lovers.

Before Amanda could even put the plate down on the side table, Max snatched one. He bit into it with enthusiasm. His chewing slowed, and he struggled to swallow. He cleared his throat. "These aren't like the other ones."

"What do you mean?"

"Well, not to be rude, but...uh...they aren't as good as the ones you brought to the station. New recipe?" He gave her a hopeful look.

"No..." She caught her lower lip in her teeth, wondering if she should do it. "I have something to confess."

A cop. A confession. Max sat up, alert. "Shoot."

She had to come clean. "Those cookies..."

"Yeah?"

She turned away to hide her guilt. "Well, I didn't make them."

"Oh. So? Big deal."

"And..." It wasn't like she'd intentionally fed him tainted cookies. Right?

"And?"

All right, maybe she did, but he'd survived and he never had to know. "Mrs. Busy—Mrs. Myers made them."

"Well, they were good. Thanks for sharing them with us."

She couldn't do it. She couldn't admit to letting him eat cookies iced with dog spit. That secret was going to go with her to her grave. "Sure." She turned back to face him. "I might not be the best baker yet, but I swear I can make us the best pitcher of Alabama Slammers."

He looked up at her in surprise. "You can? You know how to make Alabama Slammers?"

"Of course. I was a bartender for three years. I was good at it too. It was fun. I worked at a top nightclub. I made some *good* money. Met some cool people and some celebs too. Plus, the free drinks didn't hurt either."

"I could see you slinging drinks—especially wearing outfits like that. You probably pulled in some nice tips. Do you have the stuff to make Slammers?"

"Sure. I put a lock on one of the kitchen cabinets. I'll be right back."

As she turned to go, he stopped her. "Amanda, you can take the plate."

She picked up the cookies. "Now you know why I asked your mother for help." And went back into the kitchen.

Amanda unlocked the makeshift liquor cabinet and pulled out the Southern Comfort, sloe gin, and amaretto.

She heard his deep voice behind her. "Want help?"

Amanda turned to see Max leaning a shoulder on the doorjamb between the two rooms.

"All right. Go in that cabinet over there and get us a couple of big glasses. Oh, before you do that, grab the bin of ice out of the freezer."

She pulled the blender away from the wall and plugged it in.

Max stopped her. "You can't use that!"

Amanda laughed. "Oh yeah. Poor Greg, he would have jumped out of his skin." Unplugging it, she pushed the appliance back against the wall. She reached into a nearby cabinet and found a shaker. "I'll just shake them gently."

"Shaken, not stirred," he said in a bad James Bond accent. Max slid the bin of ice next to the shaker. "What else?"

"Um. I need the lemon juice. It's in the fridge door."

When she was done mixing the concoction, she poured it into a big pitcher and carried it, while Max followed her with two large glasses, into the sunroom.

He settled back into the love seat while Amanda, after filling their glasses, sat in the rocker across from him.

Max took a drink. "Now that's a lot better than those peanut butter cookies."

Amanda took a sip. She had to agree. "Mmm. That's good."

They were silent for a few minutes as they savored the drinks and contemplated each other, the alcohol quickly relaxing the both of them. Before she knew it, Max's glass was drained, and she reached to fill it again. "More?"

"Sure. Keep them coming. So..." Max's cool blue eyes pinned her into the rocker. "Did any of those *celebs* hit on you?"

"Maybe."

"And?" he prompted.

"And they are like anyone else. They're human."

"From what I've seen of them on television, I don't know if I'd call some of them human."

"Call them what you like. I had my fair share of attention."

"So you went out with some?"

"No. I had a boyfriend. Believe it or not, I'm very loyal. In fact, so loyal I consider it a fault."

Max frowned. "Why?"

Amanda just shook her head. "Never mind. I thought we were going to discuss us." She emptied her glass. The strong alcohol was starting to warm her belly and give her a nice little buzz.

Max reached out to fill it again. "We were. We are," he corrected.

"Okay, so start." She watched him down his second round of the Slammers. He was clearly struggling with his emotions. Did he need the booze to bolster him to talk about their relationship? If you could call it that.

Max grimaced and shifted uncomfortably. "I don't know where to begin."

"Okay, so I'll start. Look..." She crossed her legs and with one foot put the rocking chair in motion while she tried to organize her thoughts into words.

Maybe the Alabama Slammers weren't the best idea. Her thinking was a bit fuzzy. *What the hell, here goes...*

"I don't know if I can deal with your indecisions. I'm having a hard enough time dealing with my own. I don't know what's going to happen in the future. I don't know where I'm going to end up. I don't know what I want to do when it comes to staying here in Manning Grove or heading back to Miami."

"So what you're saying is that you expect me to accept your indecision but you can't accept mine?"

"I don't know. I'm so freaking confused. You frustrate me. My mother is so controlling. I don't need that in a man."

"I can't help it. That's me. That's why I'm a cop. I don't know if I can ever change that." He shrugged matter-of-factly. "Genetic makeup, if you will."

"Bull. That's the easy way out. Genetic makeup...*please*."

"So don't believe me. But believe this...I told you to keep that outfit on. And you did. I think you like it, and you just don't want to admit it."

Was he right? Did she need someone who was controlling in her life at all times?

"Give me a break. Maybe I kept this outfit on because I didn't think you were worth changing for."

Max chuckled at her blatant lie. He filled his glass for the third time. He emptied the pitcher. "Look, let's just have a compromise. Another truce? Let's agree to take it slow and see where this goes."

"Another truce?"

"How about we call it a compromise this time, since we failed at our so-called earlier truce. I promise to try not to be so controlling—"

"Bossy, overbearing—"

"Okay, okay. And you give Manning Grove—and me—a chance."

"Max, I can't promise that I will stay in this town. But, how's this: I won't say that I am definitely leaving."

"Good enough. Now about my mother—"

"No, that's not in the 'compromise.' I get to spend as much time with your mother as I want."

Max leaned back with eyes hooded, his lips pressed together.

"Max," Amanda warned. "Do you want to fuck this up before it's even started?"

"No. But I want you to discourage her if she starts picking out invitations and cummerbund colors."

She tried to appear serious. "Agreed."

"If she starts taking you on a three-hour drive to Harrisburg to Babies "R" Us, I want you to escape and head toward the nearest phone to dial 9 1 1."

Amanda's lips twitched. "I do have a cell."

"And anything we do in private is off limits from her ears."

"Deal."

"And..."

"Enough, Max. I get the picture. I won't tell her how horny you make me. And how you make me cry out when I orgasm."

Max's grin twisted. "Well, you can tell me instead."

"Do you want me to make another pitcher?"

Max shook his head and stretched out a hand. "C'mere. You're too far away."

She studied him a moment before getting out of the rocker and joining him on the love seat. She settled onto his lap. "Better?"

Max curled his arms around her and pulled her tighter against his chest. "You bet."

She laid her head on his shoulder and snuggled her nose into his neck. She could feel his strong pulse against her cheek.

It felt so good to be in his arms. She circled his tattoo with her finger. Semper Fi. Mary Ann had made sure to tell Amanda that it meant "always faithful."

"Did you always want to be a cop?"

He had one hand on her hip and the other on her thigh, rubbing it slowly back and forth. "Yes."

She waited a moment, and when he said nothing further, she prodded. "Why?"

His deep voice resonated through his chest. "I was always in awe of my grandfather and my father. That's why I followed in their footsteps. That's why all three of us did. The Marines first, to serve our country, and then the police department, to serve our community."

"To protect and serve, huh?"

The pride exuded from his words. "It's the Bryson family motto."

She moved her nose up to nuzzle him behind the ear. "Well, you can protect and serve me anytime."

"I'd planned to since the minute you bitched me out in that parking lot when you first came to town."

She raised her head, pushing herself up with a palm against his chest. "You were only trying to get into my pants."

"True..." he said slowly.

Amanda grabbed a nearby decorative pillow and whacked him.

"Hey! You didn't let me finish. True, but when you saw me in my uniform, you just wanted a big ol' piece of this bad boy." He opened his arms wide as if offering himself to her.

Amanda whacked him again. "Yeah, right."

"You can't say you didn't want this." He reached out, and his long fingers cupped her face as he leaned in to kiss her. It was only a slight brush, leaving her wanting more.

"No, I didn't."

"Would you have kissed me if I had torn up the ticket?"

"No."

"Liar."

"For twenty-five bucks? Get real. I wanted to take out that retractable metal stick you carry and beat you over the head."

Max laughed. "You mean my ASP baton?"

"Whatever."

"Only because you were sexually frustrated."

"You wish."

He poked her side gently. "Admit it."

"No."

"C'mon."

"Okay. You're right. I was sexually frustrated because I couldn't jump your bones right there in the middle of town, in the *free* parking lot on the pavement amid a bag of spilled dog toys, while Greg looked on. Satisfied?"

His smile widened. "Yep."

"Good. Now kiss me again." She grabbed the back of his head and pulled it down until their lips were a breath apart. "And do it like you mean it this time."

The light peck was easily forgotten as he claimed her mouth with his, crushing her to him. This was what she had been waiting for. She groaned into his mouth, tangling her tongue with his. She felt a twinge and wiggled her hips in his lap, feeling his body harden.

He pulled back slightly. He ran a finger under the edge of her skintight black pants. "You know, I've drunk too much to drive. I guess I'll have to stay put until I sober up."

"Hmm. Maybe I *should* make another pitcher to make sure it takes you a while to sober up."

"Forget it. I want to make sure you remember everything I do to you."

"You're right. I want to make sure you *can* do everything to me."

"So we're going to seal this new compromise with another kiss?"

"No, even better..." Amanda unfolded herself from his lap to take his hand and lead him upstairs.

As the steps creaked underneath him, she whispered, "We need to be quiet."

At the top of the stairs, he answered, "I'm not sure that will be possible. You squeal like a pig."

Amanda stifled a laugh and poked him in the ribs with her elbow.

"Ow!"

"Shh!" She pulled him into the master bedroom and shut the door quickly behind them.

She leaned against the door and watched him rub his ribs. His fingers were long and strong, and she knew what they could do to her, how undone she could become. Her stomach fluttered at the thought.

He splayed himself over the bed and held out a hand to her. "I feel like a teenager trying to have sex in my parents' house and not get caught."

Amanda reached behind her to turn the lock. "Are you going to be able to stay quiet?" she asked him.

A wicked smile crossed his face. "Oh yeah. But I doubt you'll be able to."

"I hear a challenge."

He laughed quietly. "You betcha. Are you game?"

She peeled off the pink tank top, over her shoulders, over her head, and then tossed it to the floor.

Her lips curled into a grin as she brought up her hands to caress her breasts. She held the heavy weight of them and squeezed. She purposely kept her gaze averted from Max as she plucked both of her nipples, then twisted the hard peaks between her fingers. She let one go so her free hand could slide down her belly and dip into her shorts. She flung her head back as she touched her own wetness, her heat.

Impatient, she wiggled out of her shorts, then leaned back against the bedroom door, spreading herself wide with her fingers so Max could see how ready she was. She slowly rubbed her thumb over her clit, circling it, making it swell.

She still hadn't looked at him. She concentrated on herself, driving herself crazy. Because if she did that, she knew full well that it was driving him crazy too. She licked her lips, then peered at him through her thick mane of hair.

Yes.

His gaze was glued to her. He was slowly stroking himself over his jeans. His T-shirt was already gone, and his tanned skin wore a slight sheen, detectable even in the low light.

"I'm so ready for you," he told her, his voice low and raspy.

"I see that."

"Are you ready for me?"

She closed the short distance to the bed and climbed up and over him to straddle his waist. "I'm not sure. Do you want to test me to make sure?"

He slid a finger between her plump pussy lips. The shine on his skin left neither of them without any doubt. She was wet and ready.

She reached behind herself to unsnap and unzip his jeans. "These need to go."

Within seconds, his shoes and socks had been kicked off, and he slithered out of his pants and boxer briefs without unseating Amanda from his waist.

"I want you on top." His words were heavy with need.

"That was the plan."

"Oh, it was, was it?"

She shifted back, the crown of his cock just barely teasing her opening. He twitched his cock against her, and in a quick lift of her hips, she seated him deep inside her.

Max let out a long, low hiss. He wrapped his fingers around the curves of her hips. Amanda closed her eyes, savoring the sensation of being completely filled. They fit perfectly together.

The pressure against her G-spot was intense, almost unbearable. He hit her in all the right places.

His fingers splayed against her ass cheeks, and he thrust even more deeply. She stifled a groan and put one hand against his chest, gently holding him still.

"Let me take control." She wasn't asking.

A series of emotions crossed his face. She could see the struggle within him to allow someone else control. He blew out a breath and nodded slightly. It was hard for him, but he was hard for her.

Amanda gripped him between her thighs and rode him hard and fast. She struggled to keep quiet and almost lost it until Max placed a hand over her mouth. Grabbing one of his fingers between her teeth, she fought to not bite down hard. She rose and fell on him, lifting until he was almost out of her, then sitting until he was balls-deep. He had to turn his face and smother himself into a pillow. The muscles in his neck bulged, and a flush ran from his cheeks down to his chest. He was fighting to not cry out as hard as she was.

She was so wet there was no friction, nothing to slow her down as she rode him, her thighs flexing, her pussy squeezing with every rise and fall. And that spot...she tilted her pelvis just enough so he hit it. Over and over. A gush of warmth ran out of her and over him.

"Fuck!" was muffled into the pillow.

She enjoyed the power she had over him. Even if it was just for a short time, she controlled his thoughts and his body. She felt him tense and she stilled immediately.

No. No. No. She wasn't ready for him to come.

She leaned over and bit one of his nipples. His head whipped around to look at her.

"Not yet," she warned. She bit the other one hard enough to leave a mark, and he bucked against her.

But the pain was enough to distract him. To delay his release.

"You're not coming before me."

His eyes narrowed, his hands tightened on her hips, and with a quick roll she was on her back and he was over her, looking down into her face.

A little yelp had escaped her from the quick movement and shift of power. But not loud enough to wake Greg.

"You want to come? What makes you so sure it's up to you whether you come? Maybe it's up to me whether you come or not."

Amanda grabbed the back of his head and pulled him down. She ground her lips against his for a second, then pulled away just enough to say, "Make me come."

He crushed her against him and thrust hard into her, grunting with each move. It was hard and fast and just what she wanted. She tilted her hips until he found her spot again. Her pussy got wetter with each stroke, wetter and wetter until finally...

He captured her mouth against his, muffling her loud cry. And not a second later, she was capturing his release within her. After the throbs subsided, he lowered himself next to her to gather her tightly in his arms. Amanda fell asleep to his slow, steady breathing and the rise and fall of his chest.

AMANDA ROLLED OVER WITH A SIGH. She stretched and reached out blindly with one hand to the other side of the bed. It was empty and cold.

She knew it. She knew he wouldn't be able to stay the night. It was too much pressure for him. After she had fallen asleep, he had probably felt the walls caving in on him and hightailed it out of there lickety-split.

Well, so much for their new compromise. He had found a

way just to get her into bed once again. Not that she had made it difficult.

She sat up. Her hair was loose and in tangles. A warm feeling vibrated through her body as she remembered that Max had ripped out the elastic band, releasing her ponytail the night before.

Her clothes still lay where she'd left them, littered across the floor in a hurry. Her heart began thumping all over again, when she recalled how he had...

Amanda shook her head. How the big, tough man had gotten his way, then moved on, back to his bachelor ways.

She pulled on a pair of yoga pants and a nostalgic *Ramones* tee and headed downstairs to make Greg breakfast. Before she even hit the last step, she heard noises from the living room. Greg was watching cartoons already.

She went in to turn off the TV and stopped in shock.

Max and Greg were both sitting on the couch with their legs propped up on the coffee table, each with bowls of cereal in their laps. And they were laughing at the antics of the cartoon mouse that was running in circles on the television.

At least Greg had a kitchen towel tucked into the neck of his shirt like a bib. It had already diverted milk and cereal from his shirt and lap.

Max hadn't left. He actually had stayed the night. And...

She stepped in front of their view. "You're letting him eat in front of the TV?"

Max at least had the decency to look at her sheepishly. "It's no big deal."

"Yeah, 'Manda, no big deal," Greg mimicked.

Amanda frowned at her brother. "All right. Just this one time."

Max had actually stayed.

"Why don't you go grab a bowl and join us?"

"Uh, okay." He was still here. And had fed her brother. She walked into the kitchen, not sure if she should be happy or suspicious.

She looked at the variety of cereal boxes that had been pulled out of the cabinet and were strewn across the counter. The utensil drawer was still wide open. She opened the refrigerator. A gallon jug of milk sat empty in the fridge. Well, maybe there was enough for a swallow. Maybe.

She pulled out the almost empty jug and stared at it.

He had stayed.

She frowned. *Why?*

"Sorry." Amanda jumped at Max's voice in her ear.

"You already apologized for everything in advance yesterday, remember?"

"I didn't mean to step on your toes and let Greg eat in front of the TV if you didn't want him to."

"We'll just consider this a special occasion."

Max stepped behind her and wrapped his arms around her waist. "I'd say it was a special occasion."

Amanda turned within his arms and tucked a finger into his T-shirt neckline and pulled.

Just as she thought. He had several sets of teeth marks marring his chest from her attempts to muffle her sounds of ecstasy during the night.

Love bites, she thought.

"War wounds," Max said with a smirk. He released her. "Come on. Greg's waiting."

She grabbed a fresh gallon of milk, then poured herself a bowl of Honey O's before following Max to the living room.

When the three of them were settled back on the couch watching Bugs Bunny, Max turned to her.

"Oh, by the way, I used your toothbrush."

Chapter Fifteen

MAX COULDN'T WAIT to park the cruiser, get out of his cumbersome duty belt, and strip off his uniform. He needed to slide into a comfortable pair of jeans, an old T-shirt, and have himself a beer. His shift had seemed to be never ending. Manning Grove had been quiet. Dead, really. He only had one incident regarding a lost cat and had given a warning to a teenager for rolling through a stop sign. But the long boring day was finally coming to a close.

As he turned the corner onto Main Street, heading back to the station, he heard a high-pitched, "Yoooo-hoooo!"

Max turned his head and groaned. The owner of Manes on Main was waving him down. Max pulled over to the curb, and Teddy ran up to the black-and-white, a little breathless.

Max decided to get out and stretch his legs after being cramped in the car for most of the last eight hours.

"What's up, Teddy? Is there a problem?" He moved around the rear of the cruiser and then, once on the sidewalk, leaned against the rear fender. He rested a forearm on the butt of his holstered gun.

"Nope, Officer. How 'bout a haircut? On the house."

One brow rose as he looked at Teddy suspiciously. "Does it look like I need a barber?" He brushed a hand over his tightly trimmed head.

Teddy's knowing smile said it all. Max frowned.

Does it look like I need a barber?

Barber. Amanda.

Damn.

"Actually it does. You're looking a bit shaggy. And I know why."

"I bet. You've been Amanda's best gir—" He stopped himself abruptly.

Teddy laughed. "Go on. You can say it. I've been her best girlfriend." He leaned close to tap his index finger against Max's gold badge before murmuring, "See, you know she's safe with me. Otherwise, you would have been over here pounding on my door like a jealous gorilla." Teddy gave him a sly smile as he straightened and stepped back, plucking a pack of cigarettes out of the front pocket of his shirt. He pulled one out and lit it, taking a long drag before he continued. "You know, she's been the best thing that's happened to me since I've come back to town."

For me too, Max wanted to answer. *Me too.* "Why do you stay, Teddy?"

"Why do *you* stay?"

"Family." Max shrugged. "I love it here. There's nowhere else I'd rather be."

"It's the same with me."

"But you left."

His high school classmate had gone off to New York City immediately after graduation. Teddy had left an eighteen-year-old shy boy and returned an unashamed gay man. If *that* hadn't set the very conservative town on its ass.

"So did you," Teddy countered.

"Only long enough for my stint in the Marines and then the police academy."

"Well, I did it to find myself and experience new things, if you know what I mean. Then I came back for my family."

Max shot the hairdresser a look of surprise. "But your parents won't even talk to you."

After "coming out," Teddy's parents had shunned him publicly, cutting him totally out of their lives.

Max didn't think he could live a life like that, one without the strong love and support of his parents. Even the loyalty of his siblings. And he didn't think it was fair that Teddy's parents were being so cruel to their only son.

Teddy's eyes shadowed. "But they will... someday. And when they do, they will know exactly where to find me."

Max put a hand on Teddy's shoulder, knowing it could never be enough consolation. Teddy laid a hand on top, giving it a slight squeeze. Max slipped his hand away without being too obvious.

Teddy gave him a sudden bright smile, back to his normal energetic self. "I know you're taken, but what about your brothers? You know, I love a man in uniform. And out of one too."

Max chuckled but refused to fall into Teddy's trap.

"If any of you Bryson boys are ever curious..."

Max flushed and cleared his throat. He glanced around to make sure they were the only ones in the immediate area. "Uh, if we're curious, we'll rent a movie." He grabbed his duty belt and adjusted it roughly, just to remind himself that he was all man.

"You can always borrow one of mine. Gay porn is a little hard to find locally. Or I can recommend a website."

Max wasn't sure if he was serious but decided it was safer to take it as such. "Maybe it's better that way; otherwise I think this town would go in a tailspin. You know what an uproar you created when you first opened your shop. Not to mention, right on Main Street."

"Yeah, I'll never forget those town meetings." Teddy sighed as if he was enjoying those memories.

Max knew better. He knew how hard Teddy had fought to be accepted back in town. "Isn't it amazing how people adapt once they open their minds?"

"Yeah, it took a while, but I'm doing okay. And now with Amanda here, I have a good friend to hang out with and gossip with and... Max, I don't want her to leave."

Max could hear the desperation in Teddy's voice. He knew where it was coming from. The man standing across from him needed that woman as much as Max did. Maybe not in the exact same way, but still...

Teddy dropped the cigarette butt on the sidewalk and ground it out with his shoe. "Would you follow her if she left?"

Max couldn't—wouldn't—answer that one, so instead he said, "There's nothing for her in Miami."

"Ah, but she doesn't realize that yet. Has she told you all about her mother?"

The question caught him off guard. It was a subject that hadn't come up with Amanda. And there had to be a reason Teddy was bringing it up. "Not really."

"We have some pretty interesting conversations—"

Max cut him off impatiently. "So, what about her mother?" If there was something he needed to know... If there was something that she was holding back from him, he wanted to know what it was. There was something she was sharing with her best friend that she wasn't telling him.

"I'll leave those stories for her to tell. It's not my place."

Max snorted. "Since when have you worried about that?"

Teddy shrugged and smiled. "Let's just say that Amanda and I understand each other very well. We each have our own difficulty with family. We both have our battles to fight. Speaking of family, I know her relationship with your mother threw you for a loop."

Max let out a searing curse. "What doesn't she tell you?"

"One day you'll realize how important that bond she has with your mother is to Amanda."

"Well, my mother is certainly in pig heaven right now." Max glanced at his watch and straightened up. "I have to go. My shift is over soon; they'll need the car."

"Max..."

He paused a moment before sliding into the driver's seat. "Yeah?" Max settled into the vinyl seat as the other man leaned in through the open passenger window.

"It's up to you, you know... to convince her to stay. To give her the reason."

Max's gripped the steering wheel tightly. "Right." Teddy wasn't asking too much of him.

"I'm counting on it." Teddy tapped the roof of the car as Max drove away.

GREG WAS WOUND UP. His eyes were rolling, his voice booming. His arms flailed wildly. He'd had a good day. Amanda had decided to surprise him by picking him up after day care instead of letting the bus drop him off.

Admittedly, Amanda was bored and just wanted an excuse to get out of the house. But she was pleased with Greg's reaction. Not only was the excitement stemming from his sister picking him up, which made him feel special, but also Donna said that Greg actually had learned to write three alphabet letters today.

Three. O, C, and Z.

And that was the biggest deal of all.

Donna was extremely happy with his progress.

Greg was excited.

Amanda was very pleased.

If Greg even had a slight possibility of being able to read and write, she wanted to make sure he learned. It was apparent that he would never be able to live on his own; she recognized that now. However, she still wanted him to be as independent as possible. It was something Dolores had wanted too.

So, she tolerated Greg's wild animation while she attempted to drive, occasionally dodging an uncontrollable swing with his left fist.

Two houses from home, she noticed a silver Mercedes coupe in the driveway. Her heart thumped. Though the car wasn't familiar, a feeling of dread engulfed her.

She decided to park along the curb instead of pulling in the driveway behind the unfamiliar car. The two people sitting in the car might just be at the wrong house.

If she was lucky.

She sat in the driver's seat and locked a hand over Greg's belt buckle, keeping him from springing out of the car.

"C'mon, 'Manda!" Greg complained. "We's got visitors."

"I see," Amanda murmured, staring harder at the two occupants of the mystery vehicle. Her eyes narrowed. "Shit."

Greg echoed the curse, shrieking it like a parrot. "Shit! Shit! Shit! Shit!"

Amanda frowned at her mistake. "Shhh. Greg. That's enough. We do have visitors, but I'm not going to let you get out of the car until you stop saying that word."

"Why?"

"'Cause it's a bad word. I should not have said it. People don't like to hear bad words."

"Oh. But you say it all the time. Just like fuck."

She couldn't even respond to that because, to her dismay, the occupants of the car had now spotted the gray Buick, and both doors of the Mercedes flew open. Amanda bit the inside of her cheek as she watched them climb out of the low coupe.

A well-dressed, stylish blonde and a dark Latino male.

Panic welled up in her, and she wanted to drive away. She didn't even realize that her hand had slipped from Greg's belt buckle until he was already squirming out of the car.

Amanda steeled herself and followed reluctantly. When she got to the trio, Greg was hopping from foot to foot and talking a mile a minute and, even worse, peppering the word *shit* throughout. Her mother and Carlos were staring at him with wide eyes. Her mother finally noticed her approach.

"Darling!" Anne's voice had enough syrup in it to drown a plate of pancakes. "Oh darling, how I've missed you!" She squeezed Amanda's shoulders with her red-painted, well-manicured claws as she leaned forward to give her "air kisses" that never quite made it to her daughter's cheeks.

"Hello, Mother. Carlos. Fancy seeing you here. Were you just in the neighborhood?"

Carlos moved forward, attempting to welcome Amanda with a real kiss. Amanda turned her head in time. His lips skimmed her cheek. "*Mi corazón,*" he said softly.

My heart. My foot, she thought. His pet name for her put her on edge.

Under Amanda's evil stare, the color rose under his dark complexion. He *should* be embarrassed to be a part of this farce. But here he was anyway, apparently not embarrassed enough to stay in Miami. Her mother must have pressured him or promised him something. Or someone. Anne was skilled enough to manipulate blood from a rock.

Greg was still a bundle of energy and bounced closer to the Mercedes.

"Oh, oh, sweetheart, don't touch that car. It's a rental!" Anne was waving a bejeweled hand in Greg's direction as if that would shoo him away. Amanda couldn't help but notice a new stone—more like a boulder—on her mother's ring finger. Her stepfather must be keeping her happy. And going broke doing it.

Amanda went over and grabbed Greg's hand, pinning him to her side.

"So, what are you doing here anyway?"

Anne gave her a weak smile. "Can't we go inside?"

"No."

"Well, that's pretty impolite. Just like refusing to answer my phone calls. I thought I raised you better than that."

Amanda bit her lip to refrain from saying something she'd regret later.

"We've come to take you home."

"Home?"

"Yes, since you ignored our numerous messages, Carlos and I had no choice but to come up here ourselves." She pulled a small blue folder from her Louis Vuitton purse. She held it out to her. "Here's your plane ticket."

Amanda stared at the offending item. It didn't get past her that it was a single ticket, not two. "Carlos, please take Greg over there."

"But, Mandy..." He looked at Greg with distaste. That infuriated Amanda even more.

"Do it." As he opened his mouth to protest again, she hissed, "*No discuta.*"

With a jut of his jaw, he took Greg by the arm and led him away to the front steps. Greg, unaware of the tension, was content to spend some time with his new "friend."

Amanda's gaze swung from them back to her mother, but she winced when she noticed Mrs. Busybody on her front porch, listening and watching the spectacle they were creating.

Her mother grasped her arm tightly, giving Amanda a shake. "Mandy, what is wrong with you? Why are you treating Carlos like that? Why are you treating me, your own mother, like that? We've come to take you home. We miss you. You have deserted your real family."

Amanda pulled her arm away with a jerk. "My real family? Greg *is* my real family. He's my brother."

"He's not your full brother. He's—"

"At least he loves me unconditionally. Without one single string attached. Unlike you."

Anne's hand shot out. Amanda's head was suddenly swimming, and a loud ringing deafened her left ear. The multiple rings on her mother's fingers had amplified the sting from the open-handed slap. Greg let out a panicked shout.

"I have given you whatever you wanted, whenever you wanted it. I know what's best for you."

Amanda's hand came up; she placed her cool palm to her hot cheek, soothing the burn. Her mother had hit her! Greg was calling out her name and struggling against Carlos.

Somewhere in the back of her spinning mind, she heard Mrs. Myers' screen door slam. "Fuck!"

"Mandy! I'm sorry. But I'd do it again if it would knock some sense into you. You don't belong here. You've got the rest of your life ahead of you! Do you want to be tied down with a re—"

"Don't. Don't you dare."

Amanda looked at her mother in disgust. Her nostrils flared with each breath she took, the only sign of her struggle to keep her composure. She fought back the tears that welled up. Her mother had hurt her. Physically. Emotionally.

Her mother had disappointed her once again.

Lights flashing and sirens blaring, a black-and-white raced up the road, sliding to a stop across the end of the driveway. The door flung open, and Marc raced over to her and her mother, stepping between them.

"Amanda! Are you okay?"

Amanda nodded, at a loss of words. She was briefly aware of Marc reaching up and speaking into the radio on his shoulder. There were chaotic voices around her, and she couldn't tell who was saying what.

Not only was the situation bad—and embarrassing that it was being carried out on her front lawn—but it was getting worse by the moment as another cruiser squealed to a stop. Next it would be the media.

Max rushed up to her. He took Amanda by the shoulders and spun her to face him. He tucked a finger under her chin, tilting it to get a better look.

Max's expression hardened, and his ice-blue eyes bounced over to Greg, then landed on Carlos. His back grew ramrod straight.

"Did he do this to you?"

Amanda wordlessly shook her head.

"Are you sure..."

Anne pulled away from Marc to face Max. "I did it, Officer. She's my daughter, and I have every right to hit her."

"You have every right to go to jail for domestic violence."

"For smacking my own daughter? I've come to take her home with me, and she is being obstinate."

"Is that right?" Max grit out.

"Yes. Mandy... Darling. I took care of everything. You'll see. You will be much happier. I talked to that lawyer... What's his name? Mr. Wells. He's making arrangements to find the boy a good facility as we speak."

"You did what?" Amanda shook her head, unable to absorb her mother's words.

"Greg will be well taken care of. He won't want for anything. And you will come home, and we will announce your engagement to Carlos."

"Her what?" Max's brows lowered as he looked at Carlos,

who suddenly looked a bit paler, then back at Amanda. He then turned his attention back to Anne. "I don't think so, ma'am. I am not letting her go."

"What do you mean?" She looked from Amanda and back to Max, seeing the arm he had wrapped protectively around her shoulders. "Mandy? Have you been sleeping with this...this *police officer?*" When Amanda didn't confirm or deny, her mother gasped. "Are you kidding me? You would give up all that Carlos and his family could give you... for this? For this blue-collar worker?" Anne spit out *blue-collar worker* as if the words alone had dirtied her tongue.

"What does that have to do with anything, Mother? You'd rather me marry a man I don't love just because his family is wealthy. You want me to be just like you?"

Carlos stepped next to her mother, looking nervously at the two larger men. Men who were also cops. "Anne."

"Carlos, I have this under control."

His accent was thicker than ever, something Amanda recognized that happened when he was lying or nervous. "Anne, I think we should leave."

"I'm not leaving without my daughter."

Max stepped in front of Amanda, shielding her from their view. "You have no choice. If you don't get out of here right now, I am dragging the both of you to jail."

Amanda moved from behind Max to face Anne. Anne was her mother; she needed to take control of this situation. For once in her life, she realized she needed to be in control. Her. Not anyone else. "Mother, you should go."

"Mandy, please. Don't throw your life away. I only want what's best for you."

Amanda closed her eyes, then threw back her head, letting out a short, bitter laugh. She focused once again on the older woman.

"Wow, Mother, you have a funny way of showing it," she said, touching her still burning cheek. "Just like you thought it was best that I didn't go to Dad's funeral? You thought it was best not to tell me that Dad died until *after* his funeral, so I missed it?" She confronted Carlos. "Did you know that, Carlos? Did you know that this woman was capable of that?"

Carlos sadly shook his head. "No. *Lo siento, mi corazón.*"

"I'm sure you are," she bit off with a mocking tone. "And don't call me that."

Max studied Amanda's face, concern crossing his brow. "Do you want me to arrest her? I have every right to. She left a mark."

"No." It was then that she realized that Marc and Greg had disappeared. Marc's cruiser was gone. The driveway was no longer blocked. The interlopers could leave.

"Ma'am, time to go. And I'll give you this warning—if I see you here again without Amanda's permission, I will arrest you. And that is a promise."

Amanda watched as her shocked mother took Carlos's arm for support. He helped her over to the car and into the driver's seat. As he straightened up, Amanda called out, "Carlos!"

He looked at her.

"*Nunca deseo ver o oír de usted otra vez.*"

He tilted his head in acceptance before sliding into the passenger seat.

Amanda stood frozen in place until the silver Mercedes disappeared down the street.

She let out a shaky sigh. Suddenly she was trembling uncontrollably. She hated it. She hated the overwhelming fury she was feeling right now. She hated that her mother could do this to her.

It wasn't even the slap as much as the gall of thinking that Amanda would drop everything and come running when called. Or when bought. Money wasn't everything. Amanda was learning that.

Max reached out to envelop her in his arms, tucking her head under his chin. She rested against his dark blue uniform, soothed by his solidness and by his scent. She breathed deeply, trying to control her emotions.

His voice was low and slightly husky in her ear. "What did you tell him?"

She softened as he stroked a gentle hand down her back. "That I never want to see or hear from him again." His hand paused, and he disengaged himself from her.

"Let's go inside. There are too many eyes around here."

She agreed and followed him into the house.

As he closed the door behind her, he took her hand in his and led her over to the couch.

"What happened to Greg?"

"He's with Marc."

"Oh." They sank onto the couch. Amanda leaned into him, needing to feel his energy. She was sapped. "What are they doing?"

"Greg's doing a ride-along."

"A what?" It dawned on her what he was talking about. Worry flickered through her and creased her brow. "Is that safe?"

"Amanda, this is Manning Grove. Not Miami."

It was selfish of him, but he was glad Marc took Greg with him. Max wanted to be alone with her. The ride-along was safe. Marc was responsible and a good cop; it was perfectly safe.

Even so, he hoped it ended up being a slow evening in Manning Grove.

He turned his attention back to Greg's sister. Her cheek was still red as well as a bit inflamed. "Are you okay? Do you want some ice?"

Amanda lifted fingers to her cheek. "I'm fine. Don't you need to get back to work?"

"I was actually finishing up my shift. But right now I want to talk to you."

"Whenever you say that, we end up naked."

He chucked softly. She was right. "Unfortunately, this time will have to be different. I'm still on duty until I return the car and get out of my uniform." He brushed a wayward strand of auburn hair away from her face to tuck it behind her ear. "Why did they come here in person?"

"I refused to take either of their calls."

"Who was that?"

Amanda understood what he was asking. "An ex-boyfriend."

"Your mother said something about an engagement."

"In her dreams."

"Why would she want you to marry Carlos?"

"Because Carlos and his family have money. Not just money, but *old* money. And I guess my mother thinks money is more important than love. No, I don't guess; I know."

It almost surprised Max that she didn't agree with her mother's philosophy. But then he couldn't help but notice how much she had matured since coming to Manning Grove—it seemed as though months had put years on her. "You dated?"

"All through college. But after I caught him cheating with my best friend twice, I kicked him to the curb."

Carlos didn't deserve her. Max might not be rich and he may be a "blue-collar" worker—the witch had said it like it was an insult—but anyone could see that he was a better catch than Carlos.

If he was trying to be caught.

He changed his train of thought. "What's your degree in?"

"Business administration. That was something else my mother controlled. She insisted I major in that. She hoped I'd meet a rich businessman." She sighed. "I wanted to major in fashion design. That's why I ended up bartending after college instead of taking advantage of my degree. It was fun and it pissed her off."

That was so like his Amanda, giving as good as she got. *His* Amanda...

"So, would you have come to your father's funeral if you had known?"

"Of course! We may have never been close—one more thing my mother controlled—but he was still my father. When I found out that my mother never gave me the message... I'm sure Dolores expected that a mother would tell her daughter that her father died. It wasn't Dolores's fault."

"You know, after all my years of being a cop and a Marine, I've never heard anything so downright cruel."

Amanda turned wide, glassy eyes to him. "It was, wasn't it?"

His heart skipped a beat. He reached out and, with his thumb and forefinger, carefully turned her face up to his.

This woman took his breath away.

He searched her face.

"Max," she whispered.

He brushed his lips across hers. And again. Her lips parted, giving him complete access. Their tongues danced with each other. He buried his hands in her hair in his attempt to bring her even closer.

He kissed the corners of her mouth, then pulled back slightly before he totally lost his head. "I'm glad to hear that love is more important to you than money," he murmured against her lips.

"And why is that?"

How could he answer that? Why was he getting so soft? He couldn't. He wasn't.

Max disentangled their arms and jumped to his feet. "I have

to get back to the station. I'll grab us takeout and stop back. I'll get Marc to drop Greg off after the shift."

As he left the house, his feelings smacked him across the forehead like a two-by-four.

He was done. Toast.

Chapter Sixteen

THE MELODIC TONE started out soft; then the longer it went, the louder it got. It took a few seconds for Amanda to locate her cell phone, but she finally found it under Greg's NASCAR pillow that was haphazardly tossed on the couch.

She had no doubt that her brother had been playing with her phone again. She was going to have to hide it from now on. Hopefully, she wouldn't get a bill next month with costly calls to Italy on it. Like last month's.

She looked at the caller ID. She didn't recognize the number, but she was familiar with the area code. Florida.

"Hello?"

"Sweetie..."

Her stepfather's voice was unmistakable. "Hello, Norman." She waited on bated breath to find out why he would be calling her. Especially after what had occurred the last time she saw her mother. "What's going on?"

Maybe he wanted to smooth things over. Her stepfather would do anything for Anne. Amanda just couldn't figure out why.

"It's your mother."

Of course it was. *Here it comes...*

"She's not well."

...the guilt trip. "What, is she still upset about what happened when she showed up here and tried to take over my life again?"

"No. Well, yes, she's upset about that. But no, that's not why I'm calling. Your mother is sick."

Amanda paused. "What do you mean? She looked fine when she was here."

And that was only a month ago.

"She is really sick, Amanda. The doctors have sent her home. They are out of options."

Amanda's hand trembled. She sat down on the couch. "Yeah, right." She didn't believe it. It was another one of her mother's ploys. It had to be.

"Sweetie, have I ever lied to you before?"

Honestly, she could say that her stepfather had never lied to her. Her mother had only been married to him for a little over two years, however, and she had been gone for at least six months of that time. She really didn't know what he was capable of. After all, he did marry Anne. That wasn't saying much for him.

"It really is serious?"

"I wouldn't have called you otherwise. You need to get down here right away."

"What's wrong with her?"

"I'll let her explain when you get here. Hurry home. She's asking for you."

The guilt screws tightened. She was torn. It could be a trap, but what if it wasn't? Could she live with herself if she didn't go and something terrible happened to her mother?

Would it be unreasonable to ask for medical reports as proof before forking out over four hundred dollars for a last-minute flight south?

Amanda sighed. "Okay, I'll be on the first flight I can get."

She hung up before her stepfather could even say good-bye.

She scrolled through her cell phone contacts until she found who she was looking for. She dialed the Bryson's household.

"Ma. It's Amanda."

"Amanda, honey! How are you?"

"Sorry for the sudden call, but I have a favor to ask of you."

"Of course, what's wrong?"

"My mother is very sick, and I need to go down to Miami. Can you do me a big favor and keep Greg and Chaos until I get back?"

"Of course! We would love to."

Why couldn't her mother be just like Mary Ann? Loving and open... trustworthy?

"He'll need to be picked up at day care. I'm not sure how long I'll be gone."

"Honey, it's no problem. We have nothing better to do than watch these trees grow. We welcome the company since the boys are out of the house."

"Thank you. Greg will love it. I'll drop a suitcase for him off at the day care on my way out of town."

"Godspeed, Amanda. Don't worry; we'll take good care of that boy."

"I know you will. Thank you, Ma."

After a quick call to the day care, Amanda hung up the phone, then sprinted up the stairs. She had to pack three bags, one for her, one for Greg, and another for Chaos. She was already despising the long four-hour drive to the airport.

AMANDA FELT lucky to find a flight that evening from Philadelphia that was not fully booked and had a short stopover in Atlanta. With relief, she landed in Miami without incident. She hated flying.

Even though it was after midnight, the unusual sweltering heat hit her as she stepped out of the terminal and hailed a cab. She used to love this heat. Now it seemed miserable. Humid. Oppressive...

It was a forty-minute ride to her mother's gated community. The guard didn't recognize Amanda in the backseat but waved the cab through anyway.

As they drove through the neighborhood, she was startled to find herself disgusted at the waste of money sunk into the over-sized homes. She had never felt this way before. Now, living in Manning Grove, the excess was obvious. No one needed all of this to live a happy life.

As the cab rounded the horseshoe-shaped brick driveway and pulled up to the meticulously groomed front yard of the 10,000-plus square-foot home, she wondered why such an expansive residence would be needed for only two people. Two people who were hardly home anyway.

And what sickened Amanda the most was that this was one of the smaller homes in the neighborhood. The Manning Grove house where she lived with Greg was about the same size as her mother's garage.

As she leaned over to pay the cabbie, one of the house staff ran down the front steps to grab her lone bag out of the trunk.

"Miss Amanda?"

"Yes."

"Follow me. Your father is waiting for you."

"He's not my father," she muttered under her breath.

She knew it would do no good to point that out to the staff, as they probably didn't give a damn anyway. She followed the uniformed—another ridiculous expense—fortyish man into the immense foyer.

Her stepfather, dressed in a robe, greeted her with a quick kiss on the cheek and a weak pat on the back. Amanda's thoughts went to Ron Bryson's crippling bear-hug greeting last Christmas. She had felt more at home there as a guest than she did at this house.

"You made it down here quickly. If I'd have known you were going to get down here tonight, I'd have sent a car."

Her mother was supposed to be sick and possibly dying. Of course she came quickly. "Well, you said it was urgent."

"It is. It is, my dear."

"Where's Mother?"

"In bed. She's sleeping. Why don't you go settle in your room and get some rest. You can see her in the morning."

Amanda looked at her gold-and-diamond Bulova watch—so out of place in Manning Grove, but actually very conservative in her new setting. It *was* almost two a.m.

"Okay. You're right. I don't want to disturb her sleep right now. I'll see you in the morning."

Amanda hiked up the winding stairs before her stepfather could land another mushy peck on her cheek.

She found "her" room and noticed one of the staff had already delivered her luggage. Her mother had designated this bedroom as Amanda's when they bought the house, even though Amanda had never lived there. Wishful thinking by her mother. She looked around and noticed with disgust that *someone* had strategically placed pictures of Carlos all over the bedroom.

She couldn't sleep with Carlos's dark liquid eyes staring at her from every direction, so she went around and slapped all the frames facedown. After that, Amanda undressed and, with a long, exhausted sigh, crawled into bed.

She was beat.

"Hey, Mom."

"Hello! Just in time for supper." Mary Ann went over and tilted her face toward him. Max obediently leaned down to let his mother kiss him.

"Smells good; what are you cooking?"

"Honey-dipped chicken."

Max's stomach growled in response. "Wow, what's the occasion? You haven't made that in a long time. You claimed that it was going to put Pop in the grave."

Mary Ann waved a hand at her son. "Well, we have a guest."

"Oh?" Max's eyebrows lowered, pinning together. "Who?"

"Wait. You don't know?" An emotion crossed his mother's face, but she schooled it quickly before Max could get a read on it.

He glanced at the farm slab-topped table and noticed an extra place setting. "Should I?"

Had they invited Amanda over so they could feel them out on their relationship? Amanda was supposed to be keeping that on the DL from his mother. She had promised.

His father's booming voice preceded Ron into the kitchen. "Dinner done yet, woman?"

Mary Ann smiled at her husband's term of endearment.

"This boy and I are hungry; we've been working hard all day shaping those trees."

Ron stepped through the kitchen doorway and stopped. "I thought I saw your truck out there. There's always room for one more at the table." Ron turned to look behind him and yelled, "C'mon, boy, get up to the sink and wash those grimy hands of yours before supper."

Greg brushed past Ron. Max's eyebrows shot up as he looked at the younger man in surprise. He had a torn shirt, more than one smudge of dirt on his face, his hands were completely covered in soil, and he smelled like a pine tree.

Not to mention, he looked like one too.

Max's mother stepped up and began to pluck needles out of Greg's shirt and his tousled hair. "What did you do? Wrestle with those trees? Now go wash up."

Greg smiled and did as he was told, widening his grin at Max as he passed the larger man. "Max... Max! I was trimmin' trees."

"I see that, pal."

He turned to his parents, who stood next to each other watching Greg scrub his hands with soap and water, a wistful look on both of their faces. He could see their desperate desire for grandchildren.

Max frowned at their obvious train of thought and lowered his voice before asking, "What's he doing here?"

"Max, I thought you knew. I thought she would have told you."

"Amanda? What should she have told me?"

"That she had to leave town."

Sudden panic squeezed his chest. This was the last thing he had expected. "What do you mean? For good?"

"No, silly bird! Her mother is sick. She had to rush down to Miami."

He grabbed his cell phone off his hip to check for any missed calls or texts.

His phone was dead. *Damn it.* This wasn't the first time, and he was tired of his piece of shit phone dying on him. He was going to get a new phone first thing in the morning.

He was sure Amanda had tried to contact him. She would have, right? Especially since things had been going great for them in the last month.

But, no matter what, he was glad that his parents had taken Greg in temporarily.

"When did she leave?"

"Late last night. Said she was taking a red-eye."

He shook his head. "Is her mother serious?"

"Don't know, son. I thought you would've talked to her. She didn't give us many details. Said she didn't know when she'd be back. Sent a big suitcase along with the boy with enough clothes in there to last him a good month."

A month. His mother was probably exaggerating.

Max ate dinner impatiently. He felt as jumpy as Greg. He didn't even enjoy one of his favorite meals. He couldn't get Amanda out of his head. He worried about her traveling alone.

Hell, he worried about her being anywhere near that conniving mother of hers and her lapdog, Carlos.

He hoped she was staying out of trouble.

Chapter Seventeen

AMANDA SPENT the day by her mother's side. Her mother was pleasant, quite talkative, and seemed well enough to watch all her daytime soaps.

She wasn't acting sick. At all. The cook served all her meals in bed, and Amanda's stepfather came in to fuss over her every once in a while.

Anne loved all the attention. Of course, she would.

That grated on Amanda. She couldn't help but question whether her mother was "dying" like she claimed. She didn't even look seriously ill. Anne hadn't had so much as a little sniffle.

Anne had her appetite, had color in her cheeks, and certainly spent plenty of time on the phone, chatting with her country-club friends.

She drank lots of juice and took lots of trips to the restroom. Unassisted.

Every time Amanda asked her mother what she was diagnosed with, she came up with a different excuse of why she didn't know—or couldn't pronounce—the name of the illness. But she knew that it was—or at least, could be—fatal. Funny how the doctor hadn't even called once to check up on her mother. And no hospice? *Right.*

Not that she wanted her mother to die, but Anne looked healthy enough to her.

As she sat next to her mother's bed—Anne cloaked in a shiny gold nightgown like a queen—Amanda was getting edgy.

She had wanted to return to Miami so badly, and now that she was here... she wanted to go back.

Not only did she unbelievably miss Manning Grove, she missed a big, frustrating man in a blue uniform. And Greg too.

Norman peeked his head around the bedroom door.

"Amanda, there is someone here to see you." His head disappeared, and a moment later the door burst open. Squeals of delight echoed through the room, making Amanda grimace.

Her three girlfriends bounded into the room, taking their turns hugging her.

Amanda didn't fail to notice her mother's sly smile.

"Mandy! We've missed you." *Meghan.*

"We're so glad you're home." *Allison.*

"It's about time you wise up and get back here to reality." *And Darcie.*

"Yeah, come back to the real world."

As the three women chattered away, Amanda just stood there looking at her friends in amazement. "What are you guys doing here?"

"Why, Amanda, we heard you were home. You should have called us! We couldn't pass up an opportunity to get together. Hello, Mrs. Bingman."

"Hello, girls! Come, come, have a seat." She patted the plush mattress. "You can sit on the bed."

The three women plopped on the edge of the bed.

"How are you feeling?" Allison asked.

"Much better, now that you girls are here."

Amanda eyed her mother, ice spreading through her veins. She could no longer deny that she had been set up. Was it so bad that she had held out hope that one day Anne might act like a real mother? A mother who could love her daughter no matter what? Why did she do this to herself over and over? A cynical voice in her head answered: *because I am a fucking fool!*

Darcie leaned toward Amanda. "Mandy, you have to go out with us tonight. We're going clubbing!"

Meghan piped in, "You can't say no. It's Friday!"

"Yes, we won't let you."

"I've got Daddy's limo," Allison crowed. "So we won't even need a designated driver."

With all the seriousness Amanda could muster, she answered gravely, "I can't. My mother is sick. I can't leave her."

"Sure you can, darling. I'll be fine. You go and have fun."

That was the exact reaction she had expected. For once, her mother didn't disappoint her.

"Come on, Mandy, there's a cool new club. It serves all kinds of specialty martinis."

"You love those martinis. Remember when you drank four Godiva chocolate martinis in an hour and Carlos had to drive you home, because you—"

Amanda abruptly interrupted them, "Yes, I remember." Though she wanted to forget. She didn't need to be reminded of more of her stupidity.

"And Carlos is going to meet us."

Another pawn in her mother's game. She was surprised it had taken this long for his name to be mentioned. Actually she was surprised that he hadn't "popped" in—maybe her mother realized that would have blown her performance immediately.

"Mandy, he misses you," Allison pouted.

"Come with us."

Amanda's gaze bounced from her mother to her friends.

Her lips pressed together. "I'll call you guys later. My mother needs her rest."

The women were disappointed. Amanda didn't miss the fleeting glances they gave her mother, who sat up in bed propped against numerous pillows as if she was the Queen of England. More like a drama queen.

Amanda deflected the last of their halfhearted attempts on getting her to join them. In the end they reluctantly left disappointed.

When the room was quiet again, Amanda spun on Anne. She worked hard on keeping her voice calm and even. "Who called them?"

"I had Norman call the girls. I thought it would be nice for you to get together with your friends." After a pause, "And Carlos."

Amanda smoothed the comforter with her hand, then pulled it up to her mother's waist and tucked it around her with exaggerated gentleness. She softly asked, "Mother, haven't you meddled enough?"

"Mandy, you know I only want what's best for you."

Amanda unclenched her teeth enough to say, "You keep saying that, but do you really mean it?"

"Of course."

Amanda walked over to the sideboard that held juice, clean glasses, and some vials of pills, staring at them sightlessly. "Is that why you are faking this illness?"

Her mother's answer took too long. Way too long. "I'm not faking."

Amanda leaned her head over to sniff the pitcher of juice. She picked up the cut crystal container and lifted it to her lips.

The burn of vodka ran down her throat and heated her belly.

"Hmm. Vodka and orange juice." She put the pitcher down

carefully and slowly turned to face her mother. "Is that what the doctor ordered?"

Her mother looked pale at last. "Darling…"

"Damn you!" Amanda whirled on her heels, storming out of the room. The pictures in the hallway rattled from the slamming door.

She'd heard enough.

She'd had enough.

She ran into her stepfather at the top of the staircase.

"Were you part of this?" Amanda accused him.

"What?"

"Never mind!" She shoved past him, trying to control her anger. Amanda curled her fingers into a fist, trying desperately to keep herself from pushing Norman down the stairs.

"Where are you going?"

She gave a dry laugh. "For a walk before I throttle her." She paused on the steps. "And you too."

Then she ran down the stairs and out the front door.

———

MAX PULLED up the freshly downloaded contacts on his new cell phone. Amanda's name was at the top of the list. He highlighted the listing and pushed the Send button. He hadn't even left the parking lot of the Verizon store. That's how anxious he was to talk to her.

After the second ring, he thought that he would have to leave a voicemail. He really wanted to hear her voice.

But finally on the third ring she picked up.

"Hello?"

"Hello?" he echoed back. Amanda sounded odd.

"Who is this?"

"Max, who else? Are you okay?"

"Max? Oh." The bitter tone was instantly recognizable. "You're that cop, aren't you?"

That cop.

Anne. Amanda's mother.

Damn.

"Where's Amanda? I want to talk to her."

"She's none of your concern. She's busy."

His fingers painfully squeezed the phone, and he blew out a deep breath. "Where is she? Why do you have her phone?"

"She's none of your business."

How many times had he heard that from Amanda herself? But everything was different now. Things had been going so well. Or so he thought. "Yes, she is."

"She doesn't want to talk to you. She handed me her phone when she saw that it was you calling. She doesn't want to see you anymore. She doesn't want anything at all to do with you."

"You're lying."

"No, she's sitting right here. Amanda, do you want to talk to him?" There was a slight pause on the other end. "She's saying no. She's home to stay now. She's where she belongs."

"I want to hear it from her lips."

"She refuses to talk to you. What's that, darling?" A longer pause this time. "Oh, she wants me to tell you that she is announcing her engagement to Carlos."

Max hesitated. He must not have heard correctly. "She wouldn't desert Greg."

"We'll make sure he goes to a good home."

A good home? Like a shelter animal? "She wouldn't want..."

"Leave us—her—alone! She doesn't want you anymore. You're not good enough for her."

The connection was cut off.

With an explosive curse, Max violently threw his new phone

down on the floorboard. He smashed it with the heel of his boot into tiny jagged pieces.

EVERYTHING AROUND HER WAS OVERSIZED. Oversized homes, oversized cars, and oversized tastes in general.

All unnecessary. All unneeded, except to impress.

She continued to walk for blocks through the winding streets of the gated community, trying to work out the anger she felt for her own mother.

She had fallen for her mother's games. Stupid little fool.

She thought of Mary Ann and how selfless the woman was. Willing to help her anytime she asked. No strings. No games. Everything honest and up front.

Why couldn't she have had a mother like that?

She thought about the difference between Carlos and Max.

Carlos: Disloyal. Spoiled. Wishy-washy. Easily manipulated by Anne.

Max: Solid. Powerful. Not an indecisive bone in his body. Okay, except when it came to them. But it had gotten better since they had called a "truce" last month.

He stepped right in whenever she needed him. He was a natural when it came to dealing with Greg. And Greg loved him too.

Greg loved him *too*.

She stopped walking and closed her eyes. *What the hell.* She loved him. She loved Max! She didn't want to live without him.

She was going to go back to the house, pack her stuff, and go home.

Home.

To Manning Grove.

To Greg.

To Max.

There was nothing here for her in Miami anymore.

Nothing she wanted. Or needed.

Amanda quickly returned to the house. Every determined step she took was a step closer to going home.

As she quietly entered the house, she passed the sitting room. Her mother was there. Out of bed. In perfect makeup, dripping with jewelry, and wearing an elegant designer pantsuit, sipping what looked like... a Cosmo!

She stepped into the room, the anger bubbling back up. "Feeling better, Mother? Miraculous recovery?"

"Darling, you know I did it all for you. I was desperate. I had to get you out of that... that place. I needed to remind you of what you're missing. To remember what you had given up. I don't want you to go back. Look at what all that you can have here. Money, friends, a home with us, anything you want..."

Anything she wanted.

She wanted nothing from her mother. Nothing at all.

Everything she wanted was up north.

Amanda cut off her speech. "Is that my cell?"

Anne looked down at the phone in her hand, almost as if she was unaware that she was still holding it. Her mouth silently opened and closed before answering. Then she lifted her chin like a defiant child. "It rang and I answered it."

"Who was it?" she asked warily. "Was it Max?" She snagged the phone from between her mother's fingers and checked her call log. It was.

"Is that his name?"

"What did you say to him?"

"I told him the truth: that you're home now. That he's not good enough for you."

"Mother, you wouldn't know the truth if it bit you in the ass."

Anne ignored her outburst. "I told him that you went back to Carlos."

Amanda sank down on the sofa. She dropped her head in her hands. "And what did he say?"

Anne was silent for a moment. Amanda felt the sofa sink down as her mother sat primly beside her. She placed a hand over Amanda's as if trying to soften the blow. "He said good riddance."

Good riddance. Amanda laughed hysterically. Good riddance! Those two words would never have come out of Officer Max Bryson's mouth. He would have said, *she can go to hell* or *no loss*, or anything that ended with a curse, but never *good riddance*.

Suddenly her mother sounded desperate. "Amanda, it's true. He said he never wanted to see you again. I'm so sorry, Mandy. I realize you had a crush on him, but it's over. He appreciates the fact that you need more in your life. That you deserve only the best."

"No..." Amanda faced her mother, heat crawling up her neck. "No. Greg needs me. I'm leaving."

She ran up to her room and tossed her clothes into her suitcase. She called a cab, then scrolled through her cell's phonebook to find Max's name. She pushed the Send button.

His phone rang and rang. He wasn't picking up. Max didn't want to speak to her. She didn't blame him.

She listened to his voice on his recorded greeting. She wanted to leave a message, but she was afraid to.

Her heart ached. All at once she felt so alone.

"I'm coming home," she whispered before hanging up.

"There's a fine line between love and hate," Teddy had quoted to her once. Both were passionate emotions. She loved Max. She wasn't going to deny it anymore.

She needed him. She needed to get back to Pennsylvania.

SHE HAD A HARDER time finding a flight out of Miami on a moment's notice than she had in Philly a couple days earlier. She ended up napping restlessly in an uncomfortable plastic molded seat at the gate until she could catch a red-eye.

Amanda couldn't remember a more miserable flight in her life. Between the stomach-turning turbulence and being sandwiched between an enormous man with extremely bad halitosis and another who continually hit on her, she was at her wit's end. She guessed that the wannabe suitor didn't understand what the "evil eye" meant—that she wasn't interested. Now her "evil eye" was twitching.

As tempted as she was to purchase a cocktail from the flight attendant, she couldn't make herself spend eight bucks on a measly four-ounce drink. And anyway, she would need ten times that amount to calm her down. Or knock her out.

With her luck, she would have become belligerent and the air marshal on board would have had to take her down forcefully. She just seemed to get that type of response from law enforcement recently.

The second they landed, she tried calling Max again. Still no answer.

Either his phone was off or he was ignoring her.

Because of his job, she knew he never turned his cell off, so it was apparent that he didn't want to speak to her. Desperation and despair boiled up inside her.

While she impatiently waited for her luggage to come off the plane, she called three more times.

As Amanda dragged her bag through the airport, dodging numerous people, her bag twisted and a wheel popped off. She watched helplessly as the small black plastic, *piece-of-shit* wheel shot through the crowd, never to be seen again.

Damn!

She slammed the expandable handle back into the suitcase,

grabbed the side handle, and lugged it down to the nearest seat. She collapsed into the chair, dropping her head into her hands.

She would not cry. She would not cry.

She would not cry.

Some rude person sat next to her, jostling against her. This was the last thing she needed. She was sure there were plenty of other seats that this person could have flopped their fat ass into. Why next to her? Couldn't they see she was having a crisis?

She sat back, pushed her hair out of the way, and looked at the blurry figure sitting next to her.

Damn the tears!

She blinked, trying to clear her sight. She was going to give them a piece of her mind. When she rubbed her hand across her eyes, the person grasped her wrist.

"I didn't know what to think."

Amanda opened her mouth.

Max interrupted her. "No, let me speak. I didn't know what to think. You left Greg with my parents; you just took off. It hurt me that you could just leave without letting me know what was going on. I thought you felt something for me."

Did he not get all her messages?

"I do." Her sight cleared, and her own anguish was reflected back at her in his face.

He dropped his head and shook it slowly. "But you don't show it."

"I do!"

With frustration, he scrubbed his palm over his short hair. "I tried to call you, but your mother said..."

Amanda groaned, wiping her running nose. "I know. I know what she told you. It wasn't true."

"No?" He grabbed her left hand and raised it to study her ring finger. "Empty."

She squeezed his hand, never wanting to let it go. She wanted to make sure that it was real. He was really there, and that it wasn't her imagination running away with her. "What are you doing here? How did you find me?"

"I was heading to Miami to bring you home. To bring you back to me. I wasn't letting you go without a fight."

"But how did you find me here? This airport is huge; there are a million people..."

"By accident. A small wheel bounced off my shin. I should have known it was yours. My Amanda, always causing trouble." He gave her a crooked smile. "I'm sure I'll have a bruise."

Fate.

It was fate.

"Max..."

He placed a finger over her lips. "Wait, I'm not done." He brushed a lone shimmering tear off her cheek with his rough, warm thumb. "Amanda... I love you. I wanted to deny it... but I can't. I love you, and I want you to come back home with me."

"Home..." The thought of a real home—creating a *real home* with Max—made a few more hot tears escape. She was not a crier!

"I know you're not happy in Manning Grove, it will never be the same as Miami. It's a sacrifice you will have to make..."

"It's not—"

"But I promise to make you happy. Hopefully, it will be enough." He lifted her left hand again and kissed her ring finger. "I'm so glad you aren't wearing Carlos's diamond." Without releasing her, he slid to his knees in front of her.

With his free hand he reached into his shirt pocket and pulled out a small black box. "It's not going to be as big a ring as Carlos can buy you. But..." He opened the lid.

A beautiful petite diamond sparkled from its velvet place setting.

"It was my mother's first engagement ring. If it's not big enough, I'll buy you a larger one later."

"Max," she whispered. "It's not the size that matters." She blushed and laughed. "You know what I mean."

Max laughed too, then he got serious. "Will you wear it?"

What kind of proposal was that?

But before she could ask, he smothered her lips with his own, tilting his head to possess her mouth fully. She pushed him back down. "We're in public!" she complained in a whisper.

"I don't care. I want everyone to know you are mine. That I love you." He turned his face up and hollered, "And, yes, I want you to marry me!"

A hard tap on her shoulder made her turn her head to look at a small, elderly lady behind her.

"Say yes, dear," and with that she gave Amanda a smile and hobbled away with a cane.

He was asking her to marry him at the Philadelphia International Airport among hundreds—no, thousands—of strangers.

"Please?" he begged.

Amanda looked down at the man she loved, the man she wanted to spend the rest of her life with, the man she needed desperately... The man who was squatted down on a filthy terminal floor between her thighs.

"Holy shit," she murmured.

"I'll take that as a yes," he said and slid the ring onto her finger. It fit perfectly.

It was impossible, she thought, there was no way he knew her ring size.

Fate flashed through her mind again.

She was meant to be with this man. As much as they had fought it, fate won. "Let's go home."

He gathered his backpack, her lopsided luggage, and her hand.

As he led her through the throngs of people, she asked, "Why didn't you answer your phone? I tried calling you a dozen times."

"I... lost it."

Lost it. Right. Just like Amanda had *lost* the Buick's license plate. "Well, when you find it, you'll hear a dozen messages from me. They might sound a little crazy. I *was* having a really bad day." She smiled up at him and squeezed his hand. "But it's all better now."

As THEY DROVE into the clearing at Bryson's Tree Farm, they noticed Max's parents, along with Greg and Chaos, relaxing on the large porch swing. The swaying stopped as the trio spotted the truck.

Max parked his Chevy, and before Amanda could descend from the cab, Greg had her door open and was trying to haul her out. Chaos, with his front leg still in a cast, slowly hobbled over, giving a happy, high-pitched bark.

She squeaked, "Hold on, buddy; let me undo the seat belt."

Max reached over the bench seat to release it for her.

Amanda could rub her neck only for a split second before Greg was squeezing her tightly. "I's missed you, 'Manda! I's missed you!"

Amanda hugged him in return, breathing in the fresh pine scent of him. She ran a hand through his messy hair. "I've missed you too. Did you have fun?"

"Yes, lots of fun." He released her and stepped back. "We made Christmas trees!"

"You did?"

Ron came up and gave her a great big bear hug. "Welcome home."

"It's good to be home," she replied, really meaning it with all her heart.

Amanda saw Ron's eyes flick to her ring finger, but before she could say anything, Ron just gave her a wink.

Spotting the exchange, Max quickly faced his mother, clearing his throat. "Mom, I know what present you've always wanted the most for Christmas. And I know it's way too early for Christmas, but—" He bent over and whispered in her ear, "She said yes."

Mary Ann's face lit up, and silvery tears pooled in her eyes. With a happy cry, she rushed over to hug Amanda.

"Oh my God! Oh my God! That's the best Christmas present ever!" She stopped and looked anxiously from Max to Amanda's flat stomach and back. "Well, unless there's more you need to tell me?"

Max groaned loudly.

"Well, get busy, son! You only have six months until Christmas."

"Mother!"

Turn the page to read the first chapter of Brothers in Blue: Marc (Brothers in Blue, Book 2)

Sign up for Jeanne's newsletter to learn about her upcoming releases, sales and more! http://www. jeannestjames.com/newslettersignup

Take a Sneak Peek of Brothers in Blue: Marc

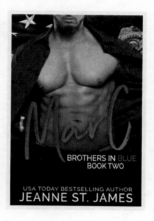

Meet the men of Manning Grove, three small-town cops and brothers, who meet the women who will change the rest of their lives. This is Marc's story...

Officer Marc Bryson doesn't believe women should be in law enforcement. Ever. When his older brother, Max, is promoted to the small town's police chief the first thing he does is hire a woman fresh out of the academy. Then makes Marc her Field Training Officer.

Determined to follow in her late father's footsteps, Leah Grant has the moxie to break any glass ceiling that stands in the way from becoming a police officer. Even if that means proving to her coach—who only wants her in his bed and not in the field—she's worthy of being a permanent member of the force.

Working in a man's world, Leah challenges Marc's misconceptions about women in the line of duty. But as they struggle to separate their work life from their undeniable chemistry, things continue to steam up and get a little kinky. These two officers of the law must toe the line after being caught red-handed.

In the end, can Leah prove to Marc that she is good as backup as well as in bed?

Brothers in Blue: Marc
Chapter One

"WHAT THE FUCK do you mean *a woman?*" Corporal Marc Bryson all but sputtered over the chief's desk and the too-tidy piles of paperwork, which were perfectly spaced apart on the spotless surface.

The chief, who just happened to be his older brother, lifted an eyebrow. "I would hope you would know what a woman is by your age, Marc. Though, now that I think about it, you never did bring any women home when you squatted at my house."

"Oh, very funny. And I wasn't squatting. I gave you money every month."

Max Bryson snorted.

"Anyway, let's get back to this discussion—"

Max cut him off at the knees. "There will be no discussion. Period. I hired her and you're going to be her FTO."

Marc didn't want to be some woman's Field Training Officer. No way, no how. Women shouldn't be cops. Ever.

"Why do *I* have to train her? Why not Dunn?"

"Because I said so."

What the fuck. Big brother says so and that's all, folks. Fellow officer Tommy Dunn wasn't going to be the new rookie's FTO because he was too easygoing, he would coddle the female, not train her for the real world in policing. And Marc would. Plus, Dunn wasn't certified to be an FTO. Though that was just semantics. Right?

Shit. Marc wouldn't give any slack to a woman fresh out of the academy. Max knew how much he opposed women in law enforcement. If she wanted to be treated as an equal, then Marc would have no problem being tough and inflexible with the rules just because she was a w—new recruit. *Right.*

Fine. But he didn't have to be happy about it.

"Let me just remind you that you're a corporal now. I warned you when you accepted the promotion that with the buck increase in your weekly salary you're getting"—Max snickered—"more responsibility."

Max was obviously enjoying this, not giving a flipping fuck how Marc felt about this new "responsibility." If his older brother could find a way to bust his balls, he did it.

Fighting this would be pointless. Marc exhaled loudly in defeat. "When does she start?"

Max glanced at his black G-Shock wrist watch. "As soon as Dunn is finished issuing all her equipment."

Marc's head snapped up and he thought he'd have to shove his eyeballs back into their sockets. "Today?"

Max laughed. "Got a problem with that, Corp?"

Marc took another deep breath. He kept playing into Max's hands. He needed to act like this whole thing didn't bother him. Otherwise, Max would ride him hard until he broke. Big brothers were assholes like that. The power of becoming chief had gone to his head. He didn't know how his wife put up with him.

Oh, that's right. Amanda didn't take any of his shit. One misstep and that woman brought him to his knees. *Whap!* Marc looked down at the floor while he chuckled.

"Something funny, brother?"

"Nope. Max, you interviewed her, so what does she look like?" He hoped she wasn't someone prissy, more worried about breaking a nail than doing actual police work. Nor did he want a beast. A woman who would look like she could break Marc in half.

"It shouldn't matter what she looks like. Get your priorities straight. She graduated the academy at the top of her class. That's what's important."

"Chief, we're done," Tommy Dunn called out from the hallway as he turned the corner. His large, lanky body suddenly filled the office doorway and Marc couldn't see the new *officer*.

Apparently neither could Max. "Why don't you get the hell out of the way, and let her through? Get back out on patrol. I'm sure Mrs. Johnson needs her cat rescued again."

The redhead shuffled his feet. "No problem, Max."

Marc shook his head and chuckled softly. He waited. Dunn never learned.

Max cleared his throat loudly and gave Tommy the stink eye. "Excuse me?"

Dunn's face paled, which illuminated the countless freckles covering his face. "I meant *chief*. Sorry, Chief." With a mumble, Dunn backed up, then jerked forward as he bumped into the person behind him. He excused himself and rushed off.

Marc leaned back in his chair and crossed his arms and ankles and waited, a frown front and center on his face.

After a few moments of no sign of the rookie, Max barked, "Grant, get in here!"

A figure appeared in the open doorway and she stood at attention, her body stiff and tight. Marc did a preliminary inspection, starting at her feet. She wore black tactical boots, the dark blue summer uniform of the department, a full duty belt that looked like it weighed more than she did, and as his gaze rose, her torso looked out of proportion. *What the hell?*

Something looked seriously wrong with her Kevlar vest underneath her uniform.

Marc jumped to his feet and stood with legs apart, pointing at her chest. "What's wrong with your vest?"

A blush rose from the tight collar of her shirt into her cheeks as she stared at his finger. "Sir, it's too big, Sir."

Fuck that double "sir" shit. Academy bullshit they drilled into you. While attending the academy, you could be at the grocery store on the weekend and have to ask a stock boy a question and you'd start and end the question with a sir. *Sir, where are the kumquats, Sir?* The teenager would look at you as if you'd grown two heads.

"I'll order you a new vest," Max said. "Just bear with that one for now. I don't want you going without. It's in our Field Regulations."

"Sir, yes, Sir."

"Oh, for fuck's sake, drop the sir echo," Marc barked. Okay, maybe a little harsh for the first day, but he was annoyed. Just a tad. This whole FTO thing was a flaming bunch of bullshit. And now he was stuck training someone who probably would faint at the sight of blood and hide when shit went down. "And stop standing in the doorway. Get in here front and center."

She rushed to the center of Max's office, heels together, fists clamped to the sides of her thighs, head up, eyes staring forward focused on some spot above Max's head.

"By the way, Grant, the corporal here will be your FTO."

Marc narrowed his eyes at the wide smile his brother wore. Then he caught the quick flick of her gaze toward him before pinning it straight ahead again. He circled her closely, looking her up and down. He checked the tuck of her uniform shirt into her pants, he checked the crease on her sleeves—it had to be centered from her shoulder directly through the patch to the hem. It was. He moved around to stand directly in front of her, less than a foot away. By being in her personal space he was testing her. Would she step back or stand her ground?

He flicked her name tag with his index finger. "Your tag is crooked. Fix it. Did you even read the regulations?"

As she repinned the black and silver tag that said *GRANT* straight with trembling fingers, Marc wondered if Max had even provided her copies of the department's Administration and Field Regulations as well as their SOPs—Standard Operating Procedures—yet.

"Sir—"

"Corporal," Marc corrected her sharply.

"Corporal..." Her eyes jumped to his name tag. Confusion crossed her face, but it was hidden in a flash. "Bryson. I have studied the SOPs, the FRs, and the ARs as required."

Well, well, well. Max was on it. Good for big brother. And good for the recruit. But she'd have to do a lot more than that to impress him.

"Every day while you're in field training expect to be inspected like this. Get used to it. And make sure you're squared away before beginning your shift."

He studied her from head to toe one last time. But this inspection was of her, not her uniform. She stood about five-six. She probably weighed a hundred and twenty pounds at best. And she was *young*. Maybe twenty-five. Young enough to think she could make a difference out in the world. She may be disappointed.

He sucked in a deep breath, steeling himself for what, he didn't know, but it turned out to be a mistake. A big one. He inhaled her unmistakable scent. Not perfume, no. It was light, floral. He couldn't help sniff a little more, trying not to be obvious. It was her shampoo, or her soap, or her body lotion. Something that caught his attention. Her dark hair was pulled back into a thick, tight bun, not a stray hair to be seen. It made him wonder how long it actually was when let down. Her thick eyelashes surrounded amazing hazel eyes. It had to be his imagination when they flashed different colors, from gold to brown to green, all within a dark outer ring. Had to be; irises didn't change colors. Her nose was thin and straight, her cheekbones high and blooming with color from his detailed inspection. And her lips...

Fuck. Marc stepped back and cleared his throat.

Max cut into his thoughts. "Grant, why don't you go and wait in the patrol room. Your FTO will be with you in a couple minutes so he can start showing you the ropes. Close the door on your way out, would you?"

"Thank you, S—Chief." She spun on the ball of her right foot and marched stiffly out of the office.

Polyester uniform pants were never flattering on anyone, man or woman, but somehow she managed to make her tight little ass looked good in them. A sigh almost slipped past his lips.

"Was it good for you?" Max asked him.

"What."

"You stripping her bare in your head."

"I didn't," he grumbled. Was it that obvious? He didn't want to check for it, or even look, but he *might* have a chubby.

"Keep it professional. Don't make me have to write you up, or worse, for doing something stupid."

"Why did she have to be so—"

Max slammed his palm on the desk top, making Marc jump. "Don't fuck this up, *Corporal*. We're already shorthanded and I need her. *We* need her. With Matt still overseas and since Chief Peters retired, there's been a gaping hole. Unless you want to work constant doubles, then do everything you can to make sure she's trained properly and is an asset to this department. As for you being stuck with all sixty days of her training, I have no other option. You're it until our baby brother gets his feet back on American soil. And even then, I don't think his head will be in the game enough to train another officer."

Once their youngest brother gets back from his stint in the Marines, it could be possible that he would need refresher training anyway.

Like it or not, Marc will have to spend the next two months as their new female recruit's shadow.

He was so screwed.

**Get your copy here: http://mybook.-
to/BrothersinBlue-Marc**

If You Enjoyed This Book

Thank you for reading Brothers in Blue: Max. If you enjoyed Max and Amanda's story, please consider leaving a review at your favorite retailer and/or Goodreads to let other readers know. Reviews are always appreciated and just a few words can help an independent author like me tremendously!

The Brothers in Blue Series:

Brothers in Blue: Max (Book 1)
Brothers in Blue: Marc (Book 2)
Brothers in Blue: Matt (Book 3)
Teddy: A Brothers In Blue Novella

Also by Jeanne St. James

Find my complete reading order here:

https://www.jeannestjames.com/reading-order

* Available in Audiobook

Standalone Books:

Made Maleen: A Modern Twist on a Fairy Tale *

Damaged *

Rip Cord: The Complete Trilogy *

Everything About You (A Second Chance Gay Romance) *

Reigniting Chase (An M/M Standalone) *

Brothers in Blue Series:

Brothers in Blue: Max *

Brothers in Blue: Marc *

Brothers in Blue: Matt *

Teddy: A Brothers in Blue Novelette *

Brothers in Blue: A Bryson Family Christmas *

The Dare Ménage Series:

Double Dare *

Daring Proposal *

Dare to Be Three *

A Daring Desire *

Dare to Surrender *

A Daring Journey *

The Obsessed Novellas:

Forever Him *

Only Him *

Needing Him *

Loving Her *

Tempting Him *

Down & Dirty: Dirty Angels MC Series®:

Down & Dirty: Zak *

Down & Dirty: Jag *

Down & Dirty: Hawk *

Down & Dirty: Diesel *

Down & Dirty: Axel *

Down & Dirty: Slade *

Down & Dirty: Dawg *

Down & Dirty: Dex *

Down & Dirty: Linc *

Down & Dirty: Crow *

Crossing the Line (A DAMC/Blue Avengers MC Crossover) *

Magnum: A Dark Knights MC/Dirty Angels MC Crossover *

Crash: A Dirty Angels MC/Blood Fury MC Crossover *

In the Shadows Security Series:

Guts & Glory: Mercy *

Guts & Glory: Ryder *

Guts & Glory: Hunter *

Guts & Glory: Walker *

Guts & Glory: Steel *

Guts & Glory: Brick *

Blood & Bones: Blood Fury MC®:

Blood & Bones: Trip *

Blood & Bones: Sig *

Blood & Bones: Judge *

Blood & Bones: Deacon *

Blood & Bones: Cage *

Blood & Bones: Shade *

Blood & Bones: Rook *

Blood & Bones: Rev *

Blood & Bones: Ozzy

Blood & Bones: Dodge

Blood & Bones: Whip

Blood & Bones: Easy

Beyond the Badge: Blue Avengers MC™:

Beyond the Badge: Fletch

Beyond the Badge: Finn

Beyond the Badge: Decker

Beyond the Badge: Rez

Beyond the Badge: Crew

Beyond the Badge: Nox

COMING SOON!

Double D Ranch (An MMF Ménage Series)

Dirty Angels MC®: The Next Generation

WRITING AS J.J. MASTERS

The Royal Alpha Series:

(A gay mpreg shifter series)

The Selkie Prince's Fated Mate *

The Selkie Prince & His Omega Guard *

The Selkie Prince's Unexpected Omega *

The Selkie Prince's Forbidden Mate *

The Selkie Prince's Secret Baby *

About the Author

JEANNE ST. JAMES is a USA Today bestselling romance author who loves an alpha male (or two). She was only thirteen when she started writing and her first paid published piece was an erotic story in Playgirl magazine. Her first romance novel, Banged Up, was published in 2009. She is happily owned by farting French bulldogs. She writes M/F, M/M, and M/M/F ménages.

Want to read a sample of her work? Download a sampler book here: BookHip.com/MTQQKK

To keep up with her busy release schedule check her website at www.jeannestjames.com or sign up for her newsletter: http://www.jeannestjames.com/newslettersignup

www.jeannestjames.com
jeanne@jeannestjames.com

Blog: http://jeannestjames.blogspot.com
Newsletter: http://www.jeannestjames.com/newslettersignup
Jeanne's Down & Dirty Book Crew: https://www.facebook.com/groups/JeannesReviewCrew/
TikTok: https://www.tiktok.com/@jeannestjames

facebook.com/JeanneStJamesAuthor

twitter.com/JeanneStJames

amazon.com/author/jeannestjames

instagram.com/JeanneStJames

bookbub.com/authors/jeanne-st-james

goodreads.com/JeanneStJames

pinterest.com/JeanneStJames

35699200R00152